W9-BKL-726

SWEETHEARTS

M.E. Cooper

SCHOLASTIC INC.
New York Toronto London Auckland Sydney

ISBN 0-590-40239-0

12 11 10 9 8 7 6 5 4 3 2 1   10   6 7 8 9/8 0 1/9

Printed in the U. S. A.   06

Shivering

Dee felt a strange combination of excitement and shyness at finding herself in this unexpected situation, sitting next to a very cute boy who was practically a stranger. Well, this would be a chance to get to know him better, she told herself.

A gust of wind blew Dee's short hair out of place. Marc gently pushed it back from her forehead. The gesture seemed so natural, but it was so intimate that Dee felt a little awkward.

Another gust of wind came up, and Dee shivered again.

"Are you still cold?" Marc asked.

Dee nodded. "I guess I'm *not* part polar bear," she said, rubbing her cold hands together.

"Hold my paw! It'll warm you up!" Marc laughed again and took her hand in his, his blue eyes twinkling. Dee wasn't about to tell him, but the minute he took her hand, she really did feel warm all over.

Books from Scholastic
in the **Couples** series:

SWEETHEARTS

Chapter
1

Dierdre Patterson whirled around so quickly she nearly lost her balance.

"Careful, Dee," shouted Ms. Welsh, her dancercise instructor. From the stage in front of her studio, the gray-haired woman kept a careful watch on her fifteen students. They stretched, and ran, and leapt around the room in short routines she devised for toning muscles and shedding pounds.

Smooth notes of taped jazz rushed through the loud speakers as Dee, her face flushed from exertion, tried to keep up with the rhythm.

But it wasn't easy, she thought, joining hands with the rest of the class to make a circle around the center of the studio. Until this year, she'd never pushed herself to the limit physically. Beads of perspiration formed on her forehead and dampened her short hair. Her heart beat with the heavy thump of someone just starting to build real physical stamina.

"One, two. One, two," Ms. Welsh called out. "Heads up, shoulders back."

The girls kicked their legs toward the center of the room, then turned back and dashed across the hardwood floor. In single file they danced around the edges of the studio, and swayed their bodies to the jazz.

When the routine ended, Ms. Welsh stopped the music. "Very good, class," she said, putting her hands on her slim hips. "But some of you are being lazy. I want to see you raise those legs higher, and hold those arms out straight."

As Dee listened to her teacher's comments, she panted slightly to catch her breath, and glanced at herself in the full-length mirrors across the room. Her short, ash blonde hair, swept back from her forehead, met with her approval, as did her big blue eyes, and her creamy complexion, now tinged with pink from the workout.

But then Dee looked down at her body, every limp muscle and imperfection exposed by the tightness of her purple leotard. Her shoulders were strong and straight, but her upper arms could use a little slimming. And she still needed to lose an inch or two around the waist. As her eyes moved down to the reflection of her thighs, she sighed. If it were the last thing she ever did, she was going to exercise until they were smooth and slim. She'd lost twenty-five pounds in the last seven months and had only ten to go.

While Ms. Welsh talked about firm muscles,

Dee thought about all the weeks she'd exercised such will-power: The morning she'd first started dieting, and her stomach had growled loudly enough for everyone to hear in third-period class; her last birthday when she'd nibbled just two bites from the Swiss chocolate cake her mother had baked; the long string of disciplined school lunches with no more than rye crisp, hard-boiled eggs, and a piece of fruit to tide her over from breakfast to dinner.

The battle against those twenty-five pounds had been nothing short of agony. But she'd lost them. She promised herself that her chubbiness was over for good, even if it meant being constantly hungry for a couple more months. She'd never have to worry about how she looked in shorts again. She'd wear a size eight bathing suit by summer. And her mother had promised to buy her a Nikon camera the day she stepped on the scale and reached her goal of 118 pounds.

The sound of the phone ringing in Ms. Welsh's office brought Dee's thoughts back to her class.

"Fiona, would you run through the cooling-down exercises while I answer that?" Ms. Welsh asked, as she rushed toward her office.

Fiona Stone walked gracefully to the front of the class in a pale blue leotard with capped sleeves. After a moment of trying to figure out how to turn on the tape recorder, she started some soft classical guitar music and turned to face her class.

"All right, everybody," Fiona said in her crisp British accent. "Let's stretch out."

The class obediently followed her movements — touching their toes, circling their shoulders, kneeling and arching their backs like cats.

Dee wished she had Fiona's naturally slim body and graceful motions. Fiona had probably never eaten a second helping of anything in her life. The blonde girl from England had become Dee's good friend when they joined the same dance class a month ago.

As Dee bent over and dangled her fingers to the floor, she felt all the muscles at the backs of her legs grow tight. After a few more arm stretches and neck rolls, Fiona turned off the music and the class dispersed.

Dee went to gather her belongings from the front of the room. She pulled on the oversized lavender sweater she'd just finished knitting and smoothed its soft woolen folds down over her hips. Then she ran her fingers through her short hair and shook her head to make it fluffier.

"Ready to go, Dee?" Fiona asked her.

"Sure," Dee answered. She grabbed her purse and followed Fiona out into the brisk noon air.

The sun shone down with the cool, thin light of November, and Dee was grateful for the warmth of her sweater.

"I feel fantastic," she said, looking over at Fiona. "Ms. Welsh may be a grouch, but she knows how to lead a workout."

"It was a good class today," Fiona said.

"I'm so glad I don't get as out of breath as I did a few months ago." Dee had told Fiona she had recently lost a lot of weight and had never done much to stay in shape before.

"Well you look great, too."

"Thanks." Dee smiled. She appreciated the compliment, especially coming from someone who looked like Fiona.

"Were you on any special diet?" Fiona asked.

"One the doctor gave me. Twelve hundred calories a day. You know. Lots of veggies. Broiled chicken. Fish."

Fiona looked at Dee knowingly, and continued listing the regimen. "I know — no ice cream. No chips. No fun."

They both giggled.

"Dieting is the greatest torture in the world," Fiona said. "You're really disciplined."

"Just determined, that's all."

"That's a lot. I've been determined about losing five pounds before Christmas, but it hasn't done me any good."

"You?" Dee asked in disbelief.

"I haven't been dancing as much as in London. My body's used to burning up a lot more calories than it has been lately." Dee knew Fiona had been enrolled in a professional ballet school in London. For some reason, she hadn't taken it up in Rose Hill.

"But you still look so thin."

"I've put on a couple of pounds since I got here, though. Maybe skiing this winter will help keep me in shape."

"Have you skied much before?"

"In Switzerland a few times."

"Wow!"

5

"Well, I won't be going there this year," Fiona said, a little wistfully. "I'll miss that."

"I know how you feel," Dee said. "I miss Chicago. My friends anyway."

"But hasn't it been fun living in different places?"

Dee shook her head. "Not really. Moving around so much is a drag. I'd rather stay in one place and see the rest of the country on trips."

"Maybe you're right," Fiona admitted. "I guess it would be hard starting over all the time. This is the first time I've moved since I was born."

Dee thought of eating lunches alone in new school cafeterias and walking down unfamiliar hallways filled with unfamiliar faces — in San Francisco, Houston, Chicago, and then Rose Hill. Her father had been relocated four times in seven years. "It takes weeks after you get somewhere before you feel like you belong," Dee added.

"Coming here wasn't too bad," Fiona said.

"Well, you had your brother for company."

Fiona nodded thoughtfully. "That's true. Jeremy certainly didn't have any trouble adjusting."

Dee and Fiona waited at a red light and crossed the street. When it changed, they headed toward the neighborhood of stately houses where they lived a few blocks from each other. The traffic thinned down to an occasional passing car, and the streets grew quiet. Dee looked at the lawns, now dry and brown from the autumn cold, and kicked the toes of her running shoes at the red

6

and orange leaves along the sidewalk.

"I'm kind of hungry," Fiona said.

"Me, too."

"Let's go to the sub shop for a bite, Dee."

"A submarine sandwich probably has five thousand calories."

"We don't have to eat one."

"Does the sub shop have salads?"

"Sure. Come on, let's go." The two of them turned around and headed in the other direction. "Jeremy might be there. You could meet some of his friends."

Dee swallowed back the tiny whisper of protest she wanted to utter. She knew Jeremy well enough through Fiona — and through his girl friend, Diana. Woody, too, had been her friend since she'd helped paint the backdrops for a play that he'd directed last spring. But they were the only people she knew in Jeremy's crowd. Most of them were seniors, and they were the most popular group at Kennedy High. Forgetting how good she looked now that she'd lost so much weight, Dee felt a momentary attack of shyness.

"Come on," Fiona urged as if she sensed Dee's hesitation.

"I feel grungy after our class," Dee protested. "And we're not exactly dressed to go out."

"You look fantastic, Dee," Fiona argued. "And they all know about workouts." She started walking toward Rose Hill's shopping area, and Dee, though still slightly hesitant, went along. "I've got a dentist appointment at two o'clock," Fiona added. "We've got to hurry so I can get back home in time to have Mum take me there."

Just as Dee started asking Fiona more about Switzerland, a car came up behind them and blasted its horn so loud they both jumped.

"Hey, Fiona!" a boy shouted from a red MG convertible. He and another boy were zooming along the street with the top down, the wind whipping through their hair. The driver slowed down beside the girls to wave.

"Ted! Marc!" Fiona shouted and waved back at them. "Aren't you freezing?"

"No way! It feels great," the driver yelled as he sped up again and drove away.

Dee watched the MG get smaller and smaller until it became a red speck and turned the corner in the distance.

"That was Ted Mason," Fiona explained. "He's something called the quarterback on the JFK football team." Fiona was still a little hazy on American terms.

"The quarterback, wow! He was the one driving?"

"Yeah, he's rather nice-looking, isn't he?"

Dee grinned at her friend. "So was the one beside him."

"That was Marc Harrison."

"A senior?"

"No. A junior. He's first string on the football — oh sorry, the *soccer* — team, and he and Ted played baseball in the same league last summer. I just heard he and Jenny Woods broke up after going together for a whole year. She's supposed to be really upset about it."

8

"I don't think I know her."

"She's in our class. You've probably seen her. She's really pretty. Tall. Blonde. She lives next door to Peter Lacey. They're pretty friendly."

"Hmmm." Dee tried to place her, but still wasn't sure she knew who she was.

"You'd like Ted and Marc," Fiona said. "If we're lucky, they'll be at the sub shop and you can meet them."

Dee felt a twinge of shyness again. But she did want to get to know more people at Kennedy. In spite of the fact that she felt sweaty and tired from her work-out, she held back her protests, and hurried off along with Fiona.

Chapter 2

"There's Ted's MG," Fiona said, nodding toward the parking lot as she and Dee approached the sub shop.

Just above their heads hung a huge wooden sign shaped like a submarine sandwich. Tomatoes, cheese, and lettuce hung in delicious abundance over the edges of the bread, tempting anyone who passed by.

Dee glanced at the sign and wished she could indulge in such high-calorie wickedness. Maybe by summer, she thought, and reached to open the sub shop's heavy wooden door. The minute she and Fiona walked inside, they were assaulted by a blast of Bruce Springsteen's music.

Long picnic tables were lined up in rows down the center of the sub shop, and more intimate booths with wooden seats took up the edges of the room. Dee and Fiona went to the counter, gave their orders for salads, and waited for their lunches to appear from the kitchen. As the cook handed them their food, they heard Jeremy shouting to them from across the room.

"Hey, Dee! Fiona!" Jeremy waved his arms to flag them down. "Over here! Have you just come from your exercise class?" he asked.

"Can't you tell? Ms. Welsh worked us half to death today," Fiona answered.

"It's good for you," Jeremy grinned as he scooted down the wooden bench to make room for Dee and Fiona at the end of the table. Dee saw Marc and Ted at the other end and smiled at them.

"Do you know everybody here, Dee?" Jeremy asked.

"Not really."

"You know Woody, don't you?"

Dee nodded and Jeremy worked his way around the table and introduced Dee to everyone else: Sasha, Brenda, Laurie Bennington and Dick Westergard, Ted Mason.

When Dee finally said hello to Marc Harrison, she thought he looked even better than he had in Ted's MG. A tousle of brown hair fell over his forehead, above eyes that were an incredibly bright blue. His cheeks were still ruddy from riding around in the convertible in the cold, and the corners of his mouth seemed to turn up in a perpetual smile of amusement.

"Here's Pheeberooni!" Woody said as Phoebe walked over to their table.

She set down her tray and squeezed in between

Dee and Jeremy. "Have any of you seen Michael?" she asked.

"He didn't show up for rehearsal this morning," Woody said.

"What rehearsal?" Brenda asked.

"For the Arts Fair," Woody answered, "to raise money for the art and theater departments. We're going to have live music to make it a real event."

Phoebe's forehead wrinkled in a frown. "Michael was all excited about the rehearsal when we went out last night. I can't imagine why he didn't show up. It's not like him to disappear without calling me."

"Don't worry, Pheeb," Woody said. "He'll turn up sooner or later."

"How do you like Ms. Welsh's dancercise class?" Sasha asked Dee and Fiona.

"It's great," Dee answered.

"I've heard that she's a terrific teacher," Sasha said. "I've thought about signing up for it."

"It's a good way to stay in shape," Fiona said.

"I could use some exercise." Phoebe gave her stomach a pat. "Too many subs, and winter is coming, so no more outdoor sports for me."

"The ones who have to stay in shape are those guys." Brenda pointed to Ted and Marc at the end of the table.

"Ready for the football game tonight?" Fiona asked Ted.

"Of course," Ted answered.

"If we don't beat East High, we're in trouble," Marc added.

"I've heard they're the worst team in our county," Laurie agreed.

"My sportswriter doesn't even want to cover the game because he thinks it'll be so boring," Sasha said. She reached over to get a napkin and wiped a drop of yogurt from her chin. "Does anyone know who's trying out for the cheerleader spot that opened up?" she asked.

"Trying out?" Brenda asked. "In the middle of the year?"

"Pam Singleton's family is moving to Florida, and she has to drop out," Sasha explained. "The cheerleader sponsors called me yesterday to ask if I'd get someone to cover the tryouts for the paper."

"Pheeb-a-re-bop'd make a good cheerleader," Woody said.

"No way. I'm not the type," Phoebe said. "And I'm allergic to standing around in the cold on a football field."

"She'd ruin her voice if she yelled all the time," Sasha added in support of her good friend.

"What about you, Brenda?" Jeremy asked.

"I can't," she answered. "I'm not the type any more than Phoebe is. And I've signed up to be at Garfield House two afternoons a week."

"Hey, how about you, Laurie?" Phoebe asked.

Laurie took a bite of her hamburger and looked as if she were stalling for time to think.

"Come on, Laurie, you'd be really good at it," Marc said.

Laurie took a sip of Coke.

13

"It's the first time in her life she's been speechless," Dick teased.

"She'd be great at cheerleading, wouldn't she, Dick?" Brenda asked.

Dick nodded. "You should do it, Laurie. I'm sure nobody would sabotage this campaign," he said, referring to Gloria Macmillan's double dealing as Laurie's campaign manager last spring.

"You don't even have to worry about votes," Sasha put in. "The teachers choose who wins this time because it's a special tryout."

Dick squeezed Laurie's shoulder. "I can tell by her smile that she's weakening."

"Maybe I'll do it," Laurie said finally. "I have to think about it."

Woody laughed. "That's a polite way of telling us to lay off."

"I know how to force her into it," Dick said. He reached over and held Laurie's arm behind her back in a mock wrestling hold.

"You'll try out, won't you?" he asked, in a menacing voice. "We have ways of making you, if you won't willingly agree." He gave her arm a fake twist. "Very funny, Dick," Laurie said, not looking amused.

Marc grinned at Dick. "I'll have to remember your persuasion techniques."

"Works every time," Dick said, laughing. "But Laurie'll get me back on the way home."

Phoebe stood up and reached for her purse. "Speaking of home, I've got to get going," she said. "Michael's obviously not going to stop by here."

"I hope you find him," Dee offered.

"I do, too," Phoebe said. She waved to the crowd as she walked to the door, but her face didn't have her usual warm smile.

"We should be going, too, Dee," Fiona said.

Dee glanced down at the small gold watch her father had given her last year for Christmas. "It's only one-fifteen."

"That late? I've got to take a shower and be ready to leave in half an hour."

"Okay! Let's go," Dee said.

She wadded up her napkin and put it into her white cardboard salad bowl to toss into the trash. It was too bad they had to leave already, just when she had started to relax a bit and enjoy herself. This seemed like a really nice group of kids. But she knew she couldn't let Fiona leave without her.

"Sorry we've got to rush," Fiona said to the crowd as she and Dee got up to leave.

"What's the hurry?" Marc asked.

"I have a dentist's appointment at two o'clock," Fiona said.

"Let's give them a ride home, Ted," Marc suggested.

Ted grinned. "Okay, as long as nobody minds hanging out of the car."

"That would be great," Fiona said. "It will give me more time."

The four of them hurried outside into the sunshine.

"Let's sit in the back, Dee," Marc said as they

walked ahead of Fiona and Ted to the parking lot.

"But there *is* no back," Dee said when they reached Ted's tiny sports car.

"There will be in a minute." Marc grinned. "Come on. I'll show you."

He opened the door of Ted's MG, climbed over the bucket seat on the passenger side, and settled down with a thump on the flat space behind the driver's seat. With his long legs folded beneath him, he leaned back on the palms of his hands and watched Dee get in after him.

"It's a little snug. But safe," Marc said. He reached out to hold Dee's hand and steady her as she climbed over the seat. The cold metal of the trunk felt like ice through her tights when she sat down.

"It's going to be a bit nippy," Fiona said, her British accent as crisp as the autumn weather.

Dee pulled her sweater a little tighter around her.

"Are you cold?" Marc asked her.

"A little."

"Here." He took off his letter jacket and draped it around her shoulders. She could feel the soft wool against her neck.

"Are you sure you don't need it?" Dee asked.

"The cold doesn't bother me. I'm part polar bear."

As Ted turned the key in the ignition, the radio started playing.

By the time he had driven to the end of the

block, he and Fiona were completely absorbed in their own conversation. Marc and Dee might just as well have been alone in the car. Dee felt a strange combination of excitement and shyness at finding herself in this unexpected situation, sitting next to a very interesting boy who was practically a stranger. Well, this would be a chance to get to know him better, she told herself.

"How come I haven't met you at school before?" Marc asked.

"I moved to Rose Hill less than a year ago."

Dee didn't want to explain that she used to be chubby and he probably had seen her but didn't recognize her now. Instead she said, "It takes a while to get to know people in a school as big as Kennedy."

"I guess I've been lucky. I've gone to school with most of the same people since kindergarten. I was born in Rose Hill."

"You *are* lucky. My parents have moved so many times since I was born," and Dee told him all the places she'd lived.

"What was Chicago like?" Marc asked.

"Cold. Windy. A lot worse than here in the winter. But it's a pretty nice city."

"Do you miss it?"

"I miss my friends. And Lake Michigan. We had a house right on the water, and it was great in the summer."

A gust of wind blew Dee's short hair into her eyes as she talked. Marc gently pushed it back from her face. The gesture seemed so natural, but it was so intimate that Dee felt a little awkward.

"Do you think you'll have to move again soon?" Marc asked.

"Dad says we'll stay here till I graduate at least. Once I go off to college it won't make much difference where my parents live. I'll just visit them during vacations."

"Since I've always lived here, I want to go to school somewhere really far away."

"I just want to go to a school with a good art department where I can study photography, and maybe painting."

"My mom is a painter. And my dad's an architect who loves to draw. They both think it's pretty strange that my favorite subjects are science and math. I think I want to study engineering. Or maybe computers. Dick Westergard and I have been putting together a series of programs to tutor kids at school."

"He seems like a really smart guy," Dee said. "I really enjoyed meeting that whole crowd today. I thought they might be snobbish when they were together, but they weren't at all."

"No," Marc agreed. "They're just a little overwhelming sometimes. Most of them have been such good friends for so long, it's hard not to feel like an outsider when you first meet them."

Another gust of wind came up, and Dee shivered again.

"Are you still cold?" Marc asked.

Dee nodded. "I guess I'm not part polar bear," she said, rubbing her cold hands together.

"Hold my paw! It'll warm you up." Marc

laughed again and took her hand in his, his blue eyes twinkling. Dee wasn't about to tell him, but the minute he took her hand she really did feel warm all over.

"All the exercise this morning at my dancer-cise class should have warmed me up for the whole day," she said.

"Is your class really a workout or do you just waltz around the room?" Marc asked. The ends of his mouth turned up slightly as he tried to keep from smiling.

"We don't waltz much," Dee teased back. "You know how feeble girls are. Mostly we do ankle and wrist exercises. Finger push-ups. That sort of thing."

Marc burst out laughing. "Wow," he said, "I don't know if I could survive in there."

"The class may not be football or soccer, but it's really hard work."

"I believe you, I believe you." He held out his hand in a sign of peace.

"Fiona told me you were on the soccer team," Dee said.

"Yeah. I really like it. I'd rather play a sport on the grass than in a gym any day."

"Me, too," Dee said. "I ride my bike a lot just to get outside. Even in the winter if it's not snowing."

"I have a bike, too."

Dee pictured herself riding side-by-side with Marc through Rose Hill Park, headed for a picnic by the pond. She could imagine how warm and sunny the day would be, how much fun they'd have together eating fruit and cheese under a tree bursting with cherry blossoms.

When Ted turned the corner onto Dee's street, the sound of his tires squealing on the pavement brought her thoughts back to the cold November day. She was surprised to be home so soon. She'd been so caught up in her conversation with Marc, she hadn't really noticed where they were. She was sorry to have to leave him so soon.

"It's been great meeting you," Marc said as Ted came to a stop in front of Dee's white colonial house.

Dee picked up her purse from behind the seat and got ready to climb out of the car. "Yeah, it was nice," she said shyly.

When Marc let go of her hand, her fingers suddenly felt exposed and cold.

She stood on the sidewalk and waved as they drove away. It was strange, she thought, how she'd just happened to meet Marc and Ted today, and then they'd offered her and Fiona a ride home. When she'd gotten up this morning, she'd never even heard of Marc Harrison. Now she couldn't help wondering if she'd have the chance to see him again sometime soon.

Chapter *3*

It just isn't like Michael to be irresponsible, Phoebe thought as she walked along the sidewalk toward Michael's house, carefully avoiding every crack in the concrete as she'd done since she was three. She couldn't help worrying about him and wondering why he hadn't called her to say he'd miss the rehearsal.

As soon as she left the sub shop, she decided to stop by his house and see if anyone had gotten home since she'd tried to phone earlier.

Would she ever be able to shake the feeling of insecurity that came back to haunt her whenever she sensed some trouble with Michael? She just immediately thought of Griffin and the problems she'd had with him. The feelings of uneasiness welled up and stuck with her until she was reassured that nothing was wrong.

As Phoebe got closer to Michael's house, Max,

the Rifkins' golden retriever, came bounding up to her. He stood up on his hind legs and wagged his tail excitedly, all the while whimpering little growls of greeting.

Phoebe bent down to scratch behind his ears. "Good boy, Max," she said.

Now she was sure someone would be at Michael's house. His family would never allow Max to run free unless someone was there to watch him.

"Come on, Max," Phoebe called. "Let's go find Michael."

She walked up the sidewalk with the dog at her heels. When she passed the kitchen window, she looked inside and saw Michael, sitting at the round oak dining room table with a newspaper spread out before him. A half-eaten tuna sandwich lay on a plate near his elbow. As Phoebe waved, Michael looked up at her. But immediately his eyes went back down to the newspaper, as if he couldn't believe he had just seen her.

"Michael?" Phoebe spoke out loud, even though she knew he couldn't hear her through the pane of glass.

She walked up to the front door and knocked, and a second later Michael opened it.

"Hi, Michael. Is everything okay?" Phoebe asked, trying not to sound as hurt and alarmed as she felt by his lack of enthusiasm at seeing her.

"What do you mean?"

"You look like you don't want to see me."

"No, Phoebe. I'm glad you're here."

The lack of conviction in his voice was bad enough, but the way his eyes didn't quite meet hers upset her even more. Instead of looking straight at her as he usually did, Michael's eyes focused on a spot to the left of her head.

"You didn't come to rehearsal this morning," she said, wishing the words hadn't come out sounding so accusing.

"I . . . well . . . I was busy," Michael said.

Phoebe stopped the "doing what?" that was on her lips. She wasn't going to pry an explanation from him. "We missed you," she said instead.

"Was the practice good?"

"Fine. Woody picked some great music."

"I was sorry to miss it," Michael said vaguely. "But I'll be there next week."

A brief pause passed between them like a shadow. For the first time Phoebe could remember, she felt awkward with Michael.

"You're being so weird," she finally blurted out. "Are you all right?"

"Oh, sure, Phoebe. I just had to, uh, do something else this morning, that's all."

"Do you still want to go to the football game tonight?"

"Of course."

"You don't sound exactly excited about it."

"You know I want to go. You're coming for your voice lesson later, aren't you?"

"I guess so," Phoebe answered.

She wished Michael had hugged her as he usually did when she first saw him. She wished he'd grinned at her, and started telling her about every single thing he'd done since they last talked.

"Are you *sure* you're okay?" she asked again.

"I'm fine, Phoebe. I'll see you this afternoon."

To Phoebe, his words sounded like a dismissal. "Sure, Michael. See you later," she said and turned to walk back down the sidewalk toward the street.

The sound of his front door closing behind her felt like a slap. Michael had never been like this before. Ever. Something was wrong, Phoebe was certain. And it must have had something to do with how he had spent this morning.

As Phoebe walked down the sidewalk, she thought back to the day a few months ago when Griffin had admitted he'd fallen in love with Sara Carter, his leading lady in *West Side Story*. His love for Phoebe had just evaporated into nothing. And even though he'd come back later and wanted her back, nothing had ever been the same between them.

The way Michael was acting today reminded Phoebe of that whole horrible experience. Could Michael have found someone else? she asked herself.

Phoebe sighed and stomped her foot in frustration on a crack in the sidewalk.

Once Dee waved good-bye to Ted and Marc and Fiona, she rushed into the house with a new lightness in her step. Today was the first day since she'd moved to Rose Hill that she really felt like she belonged.

"How was class?" her mother asked, looking up from a magazine.

"Great!" Dee answered.

Dee told her mother about lunch at the sub shop and about meeting Marc, then flopped down on the sofa and picked up her white cat, Lily. The cat started to purr the minute Dee stroked her throat. She felt the tiny vibrations against her fingertips. She was thinking about how much fun it would be if she became good friends with the crowd she'd met today. They all seemed to be involved in such interesting things. Dee was pretty much used to keeping to herself, doing solitary activities like riding her bike and taking photographs. Now that she was so much less self-conscious of her appearance, and knew how good she looked, she was hoping to change all that.

Dee continued to stroke Lily's throat. "It's such a beautiful day," she said to her mother. "I think I'll go out for a bike ride to take some pictures."

"That's a good idea," her mother agreed. "And just think, in a month or two you'll have your new Nikon."

Dee put Lily on her mother's lap, and went upstairs to change into jeans, and get her camera. In fifteen minutes she was pedaling her bicycle through the woods near her house, always on the lookout for something to photograph.

Today had been so perfect, she thought, as she rode along. She kept replaying the events of the day over and over in her mind like a movie. She remembered the tingly feeling she got when she first saw Marc, how Phoebe had seemed so worried at lunch, how friendly everyone had been at the sub shop, how Marc's letter jacket had felt around her shoulders. Then she remembered the discussion about cheerleader tryouts.

She was wondering if Laurie would make a good cheerleader when out of the corner of her eye, Dee spotted a pile of autumn leaves off the road. They looked as though they'd been arranged for a photograph. As shafts of sunlight filtered through the bare branches above them, they shimmered in bright reds and golds. Dee stopped her bicycle and took out her camera.

She carefully set the F-stop and focused on the gorgeous shades of red and gold. Suddenly it struck her that they were Kennedy's colors.

As Dee aimed her camera and clicked, an idea went off in her head. *She* would try out for cheerleader. Why not, she asked herself? It would probably be a lot of fun. The more she thought about it, in fact, the more it seemed like the right thing to do. She couldn't think of one reason *not* to do it. She wasn't chubby anymore. She'd look as good as anyone in a cheerleader uniform. And she'd developed enough athletic ability in her dancercise class to run and jump and cheer without getting exhausted. She might even have a good chance at making it.

Dee was surprised she hadn't thought of it before. She snapped a few more pictures and hopped back on her bicycle, suddenly invigorated from the combination of the fresh autumn air, and her excitement over the prospect of trying out for cheerleader.

As Dee pedaled home, she decided to go see Ms. Schmidt, the cheerleading sponsor, and get a tryout application first thing after school on Monday.

Chapter
4

All afternoon Phoebe felt torn about going to her voice lesson with Miss Spinelli, Michael's mother. Part of her wanted to be with Michael, to talk to him about what was going on. But another part of her wanted to avoid any confrontation — especially if it meant real trouble instead of just some misunderstanding.

She knew she loved Michael. More than anything in the world. And she wanted everything to be the same between them as it always had been. The very thought that his love for her might have changed in any way left Phoebe feeling nervous and panicky. She felt as if there was a big empty space inside her.

Everything is all right, she said to herself, as she walked up to Michael's front door for the second time that day. No matter what, she was going to try and act like everything was normal. She'd have her weekly lesson with Miss Spinelli, eat dinner with Michael's family, and go out with Michael afterward, just as she'd done every Saturday since September.

Phoebe inhaled deeply to calm herself and smoothed her hand over her fluffy red curls. As she rang the bell, she heard Max barking upstairs, but he didn't come and whimper behind the front door as he usually did. Strange, Phoebe thought.

Even stranger was Miss Spinelli's answering the door. Phoebe couldn't remember a single Saturday since September when Michael hadn't been the one to greet her.

"Where's Michael?" she asked immediately.

"He must be upstairs," Miss Spinelli said.

"Nothing's wrong with him?" Phoebe asked as she followed her voice teacher inside the house.

"No, of course not." Miss Spinelli gave Phoebe an odd look. "Why do you ask?"

"No reason," Phoebe said, trying to look unconcerned. "It's getting pretty cold outside," she added quickly. She took off her navy pea coat, lay it over the arm of the sofa, and waited for Miss Spinelli to sit down at the piano. The sight of Michael's cello case sitting on the floor next to his music stand made Phoebe feel incredibly depressed.

Miss Spinelli opened the keyboard of the concert grand. She was a tall, slim woman with dark, curly hair piled high on her head like an opera star. Phoebe had always imagined her wearing long chiffon dresses and singing arias to handsome operatic heroes. Though she mostly taught now instead of singing professionally, she still carried herself with the poise and confidence of an elegant diva.

"Have you practiced this week, Phoebe?" Miss Spinelli asked as she sat down at the piano.

"Some."

Michael's mother smiled at her. "And how much is 'some'?"

"Two afternoons after school. And today we started rehearsing for the Arts Fair at school. I'll be singing in that."

Secretly Phoebe hoped Miss Spinelli would react to her mentioning the rehearsal by explaining why Michael had missed it. But she didn't. And as Phoebe began her lesson, her confusion about Michael hung over her like a dark cloud.

"We'll start with some scales, Phoebe. Are you ready?"

Phoebe cleared her throat and nodded, knowing she was in no state to concentrate on anything.

As she sang each note in the key of A, she wondered if Michael could hear her upstairs. What was he doing now? Why hadn't he answered the door? Was he avoiding her?

"Phoebe," Miss Spinelli interrupted her scale. "Do that one again. Your voice is getting flat."

Phoebe started in a second time and tried to keep her mind on the notes. As she sang, though, she looked over at Michael's cello case across the room and felt a familiar ache.

Miss Spinelli interrupted her again. "Is anything *wrong*, Phoebe?"

"No, I just seem to be off-pitch today," Phoebe

answered noncommittally. "Doesn't that ever happen to you?"

"Not very often," Miss Spinelli answered, frowning. "Only when I'm completely distracted."

Phoebe swallowed hard. Miss Spinelli wasn't standing for anything less than perfection today.

"Why don't we go on to some songs, Phoebe? Perhaps you'll do better with them."

She began to play the introduction to a short seventeenth-century English love song she had first given Phoebe two weeks before. As her hands flew lightly over the piano keys, Phoebe looked over her shoulder to read the music.

> *Love is such a mystery*
> *I cannot find it out;*
> *For when I think I'm best resolved,*
> *I then am most in doubt.*

As Phoebe sang the words, her voice wavered, then cracked slightly on the high notes. In spite of her efforts, she couldn't keep up with Miss Spinelli's rhythm.

Finally, her teacher stopped playing and turned her whole body around on the piano bench to face Phoebe. "You really are having a bad day."

"Yes," Phoebe answered, looking at her a little guiltily.

"I can tell you're not concentrating."

"I guess not."

"Well, we all have days like that, Phoebe," Miss Spinelli comforted her. "It's only a real disaster if it happens on stage." She turned toward

31

the piano again. "Why don't we just sing a few more songs and call it quits?"

Phoebe tried a French folk song and some traditional Irish arrangements. The more she sang, the worse she got. And the worse she got, the more impatient she felt with herself for letting Michael's strange behavior affect her. She would not allow herself to get upset, she thought as she sang along, knowing she was making a shambles of one of her favorite pieces.

"That's enough for today, Phoebe," Miss Spinelli said as she closed the piano. "You'll do better next week. You'll see."

"I'm sure I will, Miss Spinelli," Phoebe promised. "Maybe I just have too much on my mind."

Miss Spinelli patted Phoebe on the shoulder. "Let's call Michael, and go make dinner."

Michael sat upstairs in his father's study and stared out the window at the gathering darkness. He could vaguely hear Phoebe and his mother talking downstairs, but he couldn't make out their words. It was just as well, Michael thought. Hearing Phoebe's sweet voice just then would only confuse him.

He had just finished giving Max a bath, and he reached down now to dry him off. As Michael ran his hands through the fluffy, clean fur, he thought back to the phone call he'd received that morning that had been the source of his trouble the rest of the day.

Just as he had been walking out the door to go to the Arts Fair rehearsal, the phone had rung.

Michael knew it would make him late, but he had dashed into his parents' bedroom and picked up the phone because he was the only one at home.

"Michael, it's so *good* to hear your voice again! Guess where I am?"

"I have no idea."

"In D.C.!"

"You're *here*?"

"Yes. And I'm going to be back every Saturday from now through December."

"That's great, Leah," Michael had said, his voice flat. He knew his words weren't exactly honest. If he were Pinnochio, in fact, his nose might have grown a couple of inches.

"I was chosen for the Washington Collegiate Orchestra," Leah continued exuberantly. "We're putting on a holiday concert and rehearsing on the weekends."

"Congratulations, Leah. That's terrific."

"Thanks. I was thrilled when they chose me."

"I'm sure you deserved it. You're a good violinist."

"You're just prejudiced. After the summer music festival, you have to stand up for me."

The image of their last night at the festival flashed through Michael's mind. At the closing ceremony, Leah had won a medal for excellence which she wore around her neck. When he'd kissed her good-bye, he'd felt the bronze disk pressing through his shirt.

He had pushed away the thought of that last kiss and had tried to keep the conversation impersonal. "What are you playing for the holiday concert?" he had asked.

"Lots of carols. Some Bach. Handel. You know. A lot of seasonal stuff. You should come and hear us rehearse, Michael. You can have a preview of what the orchestra's like, in case you're in it next year."

An awkward silence had passed between them then. Michael knew Leah expected him to make arrangements to see her. But their situation had changed. Phoebe was by far the most important part of his life now, and he'd never want to do anything that would threaten his relationship with her.

"Why don't you come into D.C. next Saturday for our rehearsal?" Leah had urged again.

"I'd really like to, Leah, but. . . ."

"Come on, Michael. It would be great to see you," she had prodded.

Michael suddenly knew how a rope felt in a tug of war. He knew he had two choices. Either he could tell Leah all about Phoebe now, and put an end to this situation once and for all, or he could agree to meet her next weekend and talk to her about Phoebe then.

He realized he had no idea how Leah would react. Even though she and Michael both knew their relationship had been nothing more than a summer romance, she would certainly expect Michael to get together with her now that she'd be in the area every weekend.

If he told her about Phoebe today, she might get upset, and it could ruin her first rehearsal with the Collegiate Orchestra. Michael knew he owed it to Leah to explain about Phoebe in the right way, at the right time. That way there wouldn't be any hard feelings between them.

"Okay, Leah. That'd be good."

"Terrific!"

"Where should I meet you?"

"In the National Concert Hall. We start at ten-thirty."

"I'll be there."

Michael had hung up the phone and sat for a moment to let what was happening sink into his head.

Ever since that call, he'd been trying to figure out how to handle the situation. He had decided to skip the rehearsal at the Little Theater because he was already late, and he had stayed home and practiced his cello instead. He knew if he saw Phoebe he would behave strangely. He was a terrible liar and he couldn't hide anything from her. Since he and Phoebe hadn't started going out until September, she knew nothing of his summer romance. He was sure it would upset her when she found out. She was still very sensitive about what had happened between her and Griffin. She'd been devastated when he'd fallen in love with someone else. And Michael was sure she would be afraid he was going to do the same thing. Leah would never be more to him than a friend now, but he would probably have a hard time convincing Phoebe that he wasn't interested in anyone besides her.

By the time Phoebe had dropped by after

lunch, Michael was completely confused about how to handle the situation. He'd thought of telling her about Leah then, but he'd held off. Not being honest had made him feel awful and he knew that his sneakiness had made him behave strangely with Phoebe. Now she was probably suspicious.

Michael looked out the window and absently smoothed his hand over Max's back. Phoebe's singing drifted up from downstairs, her voice muffled through the closed door. Would I hurt Phoebe more by telling her about Leah or by not telling her? he thought.

Michael watched a car pass on the street outside the window. I won't tell her, he decided. At least, not right now. There's no point in getting her upset over nothing. I'd never want to hurt Phoebe in a million years. Just then he heard his mother call him to come make dinner with Phoebe and her. He hurried downstairs to join them.

Chapter
5

When Michael reached the bottom of the
stairs with Max on his heels, he gave Phoebe his
usual warm smile and bent down to kiss her as
if nothing were wrong.

"You've quit early," he said, giving her a quick
hug.

Phoebe looked at him oddly. "I was lousy,"
she said.

What is going on? she thought in frustration.
He's acting completely different than he did after
lunch.

Michael reached down to pet Max. "Did you
notice how clean he is? I was giving him a bath
when you came."

"Oh," Phoebe said vaguely. She ran her fingers
through Max's fur.

"I used the dryer on him," Michael continued.
"He hates it, but it's too cold for him to lie around

37

wet for very long. He'd catch pneumonia."

Phoebe took the paw Max offered her and shook it gently.

Miss Spinelli's lilting voice interrupted them. "Come on into the kitchen, kids. We're going to make soup tonight."

"What kind?" Michael asked as he and Phoebe entered the cheerful yellow room with Max behind them.

"Lentil. It won't take long. I got it started this morning." She handed Michael two onions and gave Phoebe a few carrots and potatoes. "Chop these up and put them in the pot over on the stove. Then we can get busy on the salad."

Michael and Phoebe worked side-by-side at the cutting board without talking. Making dinner together had always been fun for Phoebe — until tonight. Right now she felt so confused that she wished she were home, away from Michael, where she could figure things out.

Michael's little brother Paul came into the kitchen. Miss Spinelli put him to work mixing kibble and canned meat for Max. Soon they all sat down together at the round oak table in the dining room.

Steam from her bowl of lentil soup curled up under Phoebe's nose with an inviting aroma that would normally have had her starting in on her dinner with gusto. But she took just one swallow and wished she could figure out a way to pour the soup discreetly down the kitchen sink. It wasn't that the soup was bad. Not at all. Phoebe simply wasn't hungry. Her stomach tightened whenever she glanced at Michael and wondered what was going on inside his head.

"Everybody have a roll," Miss Spinelli said as she handed a bread basket to Michael to pass around the table.

"I'm glad I wasn't here to see you force Max into the water, Michael," Paul said.

"Did you wipe up the puddles?" Michael's mother asked. "I went up there once and thought the water pipes had broken," Miss Spinelli explained to Phoebe. "That dog can hold gallons of water in his fur."

Phoebe tried to smile, but her mouth turned up only into the shallowest curve. She looked back down at her soup bowl and spooned out another halfhearted swallow.

"You didn't get a roll, Phoebe," Miss Spinelli said, handing her the bread basket.

"No, thanks."

"You're not on a diet are you, Phoebe?" Miss Spinelli said. She was always encouraging her to eat more, even though she knew Phoebe had to watch her weight.

"No, I'm just not hungry."

"Are you feeling all right, dear?" Miss Spinelli asked.

"I'm fine. Really," Phoebe insisted and aimed her fork toward a lettuce leaf in her salad bowl.

The Kennedy spectators were ready and cheering when Michael and Phoebe got to the stadium. They looked around for friends to sit with and spotted Sasha and Rob, and Chris and Greg, flagging them down from high up in the stands where they'd saved a block of seats for the crowd.

As they climbed up the steps toward their friends, Michael took Phoebe's mittened hand.

"If we don't beat these guys, it will be humiliating," Greg said when Michael and Phoebe sat down.

"Did you get your sportswriter to cover the game?" Phoebe asked Sasha.

"Finally," Sasha said. "I had to bribe him by offering a more exciting assignment next time. Can you believe he didn't want to come?"

"Sounds totally disloyal," Rob said.

"It's awfully loyal of us to come to what's sure to be the dullest game of the year," Greg said.

Everyone laughed except for Phoebe, who was still a little distracted.

A few minutes later, Woody and Kim arrived and sat down in front of her and Michael.

"You're lucky we're sitting near you, Pheeb-a-re-bop," Woody said. "Kim's mother gave us a batch of gourmet cookies and some hot apple cider." Woody clunked his knuckles against a thermos in his back pack.

"The cookies are from a luncheon she catered today," Kim said. "They're really good."

Woody passed the box around, but Phoebe didn't take one.

"You're passing up a cookie, Phoebe?" Woody asked, astonished. "You must have a fever." He reached up to feel her forehead.

"Hey, the guys are coming on to the field,"

Michael said, and Phoebe was glad the attention was drawn away from her.

The rest of the evening went by in a slow-motion blur.

Phoebe knew the evening seemed to be dragging on because she couldn't wait to be alone with Michael. Even if he were going to say something terrible to her, it would be better than these long hours of not knowing what was going on, and wondering every minute what lay ahead.

Michael held her hand all through the game, and hugged her when Kennedy made touchdowns. But even though he was being so normal, Phoebe could tell that something wasn't right. When the Kennedy team finally ran onto the field, victoriously throwing their helmets in the air, Phoebe was happier that the game was over, than that her school had won 19-0.

"Do you want to get a sundae with everybody?" Michael asked as they left the bleachers.

"I think we should go somewhere by ourselves," Phoebe said.

"Come on, Pheeb. I'm starved."

"Okay," Phoebe consented. Putting it off a little longer couldn't hurt.

She and Michael sat in a booth with Chris and Greg at Sticky Fingers, the crowd's favorite ice cream parlor. Soon after Greg and Chris got up to leave, Greg came back to say that the battery on his car had died. It took almost an hour for Michael to help him charge it up again. And by the time Michael brought Phoebe home, it was too late for them to talk about anything.

After a quick kiss in the car, Michael walked Phoebe to the front door.

So when she finally climbed into bed, she didn't know anything more than she had that afternoon, and she felt more frustrated and confused than she had all day.

Chapter
6

The line to the student store was so long that Dee wondered if she'd be able to buy her supplies, and still have time to eat lunch before her next class. Fiona would be waiting in the cafeteria for her. She was probably wondering where Dee was now.

Dee couldn't wait to tell Fiona about her decision to try out as a cheerleader. Fiona had been in D.C. with her family all day Sunday, and Dee hadn't been able to call her.

I wish he'd hurry, Dee thought, as she watched the student who worked through lunch every day selling notebook paper and pencils and pens. Dee counted the students he'd have to serve before her. Twelve. That meant fifteen minutes at least.

"Dee?" someone said behind her.

She turned around and looked straight into the second button of Marc Harrison's plaid flannel shirt. Tilting her head back, her brown eyes met his twinkling blue ones.

"Did you ever get warmed up after our ride on Saturday?" he asked.

"Sure." Dee smiled at him. "I even went out again later for a bike ride."

"So did I. Where'd you go?"

"The woods near Rose Hill Park."

"Me, too. Too bad we didn't bump into each other."

Dee clutched her notebook tightly to her chest and glanced down at the floor. She tried to think of something to say.

"While I was on my bike ride, I decided to try out for cheerleader," Dee said.

"Hey, that's fantastic, Dee."

"Yeah, I'm really excited. I'm going to go talk to Ms. Schmidt about the tryouts this afternoon."

"I hope you make it."

"So do I." Dee beamed at him. Everything had been going right for her since she'd met him.

The student at the head of the line made his purchase and walked away and Marc and Dee moved up in line. Dee could now see through the cafeteria door. She looked up and down the tables on the far right by the windows where she usually sat with Fiona.

"Do you see Fiona anywhere?" she asked.

Marc pointed to a table in the corner of the cafeteria. "There she is."

"I was supposed to meet her five minutes ago. I wish we could get her attention so she'd know I was here in line."

"I'll save your place if you want to go talk to her."

"Oh, that's okay." Dee was torn between seeking out Fiona and having a few more minutes with Marc. "Maybe we can flag her down instead," she said.

They both waved their arms wildly over their heads to get Fiona's attention. "Hey, Fiona," Marc half shouted.

"She didn't hear you."

"I'll try the whistle I learned in Boy Scouts." Marc pushed his thumb and second finger together, put them to his lips, and let out a whistle shrill enough to turn half the heads in the cafeteria. Immediately Fiona looked their way.

"That did it," Marc laughed.

Dee waved to Fiona and pointed to the line.

Fiona glanced at Marc, then looked back at Dee with a knowing grin on her face. "Take your time," she shouted.

Fiona knew Dee liked Marc. So Dee could tell Fiona was encouraging her to stay with him as long as she wanted. Dee wondered if Marc knew what Fiona was thinking, too. She felt a twinge of embarrassment.

The line inched slowly along.

"If I don't get some graph paper before geometry, it's all over for me," Marc said impatiently.

"Do you have a test today?"

"Yeah. Mr. Talbott's a real killer for rules and regulations. If I tried to sneak regular notebook paper by him, he'd take five points off my grade."

"So I've heard. I'm glad I'm not in your class."

"Oh, he's not all that bad. At least, if you don't mind spending an hour a day with a rabid bulldog."

As Dee and Marc stood laughing, a girl in an oversized sweater and a blue denim mini-skirt stopped in front of them.

"Hi, Marc," she said and gave him a saccharine smile. When Marc saw her, he stopped laughing.

"Gloria," he acknowledged, his voice flat.

"I don't think I know you," Gloria said, turning to Dee.

"This is Dee Patterson," Marc said.

"Oh." Gloria looked back and forth from Marc to Dee, as if she were sizing them up. "Nice to meet you, Dee. Are you new at Kennedy?"

"Sort of," Dee said. "I've been here about a year."

"I guess the school's too big to know everybody," Gloria said.

"Yeah," Dee agreed.

"Where did you move here from?"

"Chicago."

"I have a cousin there," Gloria said, then turned her head directly to Marc. "How do you two know each other?" she asked.

"From the sub shop," Marc answered.

"Great place to meet people," Gloria observed, her eyes going back and forth from Dee to Marc again.

Dee had the distinct impression that something was going on between Marc and Gloria, but she couldn't tell exactly what. With Gloria around, Marc wasn't acting like his usual good-humored self.

"Well, I'm going to eat lunch," Gloria said, flashing another smile at them. "Nice meeting you." She walked away, but instead of going into the cafeteria, she turned down the hall toward the library.

"Who is she?" Dee asked as soon as she'd gone.

"Gloria Macmillan. Sorry I didn't introduce her to you."

"Do you know her very well?"

"Um, fairly well." Marc shifted his weight from one foot to the other a little nervously. "She's friends with a girl I used to go out with."

"Oh," Dee said.

Remembering what Fiona had said about Marc and Jenny Woods, Dee suddenly had the feeling their conversation was on shaky ground. Clearly whatever had happened between Jenny and Marc was still a sore point with him.

Dee tried to steer their talk back to school and what classes they had.

"So who do you have for American history?" she asked.

Gloria found Jenny sitting at the back of the library facing the wall. Anyone walking through the large, airy room would have gotten the distinct impression that Jenny was hoping she wouldn't see anyone. Everything about her — the slump of her shoulders, the tilt of her head, the way her back was turned to the world — gave the message that she wanted to be left alone.

"Jenny," Gloria whispered as she pulled a chair out and sat down at the library table beside her. "When are you going to start eating lunch in the cafeteria again?"

"Probably never," Jenny said with a sigh. "I just couldn't face everybody."

"It wouldn't be *that* bad," Gloria comforted.

"I don't know how I could stand seeing Marc."

"If you want me to, I could walk up to him and stomp on his toes," Gloria offered, trying to make a joke.

Jenny smiled wanly. "Thanks, Gloria. But he'd know I sent you to do it." She propped her chin on her hand, and looked out the window at nothing in particular.

"I just saw him, Jenny."

Jenny's head turned quickly back to her friend, all her attention fixed on what Gloria had to say.

"Where?"

"Standing in line at the school store."

"Oh." Jenny looked out the window again. Clearly Gloria had no real news.

"He was with a girl," Gloria said, emphasizing the last word for effect.

Jenny raised her eyebrows. "Who?"

"Dee Patterson."

"I don't know her."

"Neither did I. She's fairly new at Kennedy. Pretty." Gloria saw Jenny wince. "But not as pretty as *you*," she added.

"He'll probably fall in love with her," Jenny said dejectedly.

48

"Was he acting like he liked her?"

"Well, they were standing close together, laughing a lot."

"Oh, when am I ever going to get over him? I'd do almost anything to get him back. I never thought I'd miss him so much."

"I wonder if they're going out together," Gloria said.

"I wouldn't be surprised. It sure didn't take him long to get over me."

"Well, you did tell me he was 'over you' a long time before you two broke up," Gloria said almost smugly.

Jenny nodded. "I know. I guess I'm still trying to hang on to him. He was pretty nice about telling me it wasn't working out anymore. But I can't help it that I still want him back!"

"Maybe I could find out more about her," Gloria offered. "It would probably help you forget him if you know what he's up to."

"Do you think so?"

"I know so. I'll keep my eye on her and let you know what's going on."

"You won't be too obvious?"

"She won't know I'm trying to find out for you. I'm sure we'll figure out a way for you to get him back."

Jenny thought for a moment. "Okay, Gloria. Let's do it."

For the first time since Marc broke up with her, Jenny felt a little better.

Chapter
7

Dee nervously clutched the piece of paper in her hands.

"The rules are listed there," Ms. Schmidt explained, nodding toward the paper. "Just fill out your name and phone number, sign it, and return it to me. The deadline is four-thirty today."

When Dee had walked into Ms. Schmidt's tiny, cluttered office and asked for an application for the tryouts, the cheerleader sponsor hadn't acted the least bit surprised.

"Have you ever been a cheerleader, Dee?" Ms. Schmidt asked.

"No," Dee answered, thinking about how chubby she'd been the past few years. She never could have jumped or leaped very well before this year.

"If you look in the library, you'll find a couple of books that explain some of the moves," Ms.

Schmidt offered. "And you can always talk to one of the cheerleaders if you need help."

"I'll go get a book, I guess."

"Good. And think carefully before you turn in the application. People sign up sometimes and get cold feet at the last minute. If you apply, you really should come to the tryouts."

"I won't get cold feet," Dee said with determination.

Ms. Schmidt smiled at her. "I'm sure you'll do just fine. If you have any problems, come and see me."

"Thanks." Dee put the application in her back pack and turned to leave. "I'll have the application back to you in a little while."

As she walked down the locker-lined hallway toward the library, she passed only a few people. Between three-thirty and three forty-five, the high school was almost deserted. If she were selected cheerleader, Dee thought, she'd be practicing or cheering at games after school at least three days a week. It would be a great way to meet new people.

When she got to the library, she looked through the card catalog, then went to get the book she needed from a shelf beneath the windows. *Cheerleading and Baton Twirling*. She sat down at a library table and started flipping through the pages.

She studied the book's stick-figure illustrations. The book showed how to do arm thrusts, finger snaps, knee slaps, and the other moves Dee knew were compulsory for the tryouts. She turned the page and found several kinds of jumps. She selected a cheer and decided she'd end up with a side arch jump for the optional part of the try-out. All she had to do now was practice until she got it right.

She looked out the window at the few cars still in the parking lot and spotted Phoebe bundled up in her pea coat and muffler, heading toward the Little Theater. She was probably on her way to rehearsal for the Arts Fair.

Dee thought a moment about the commitment she was making. Once she signed the application, she'd have to go through with the tryouts. That meant performing in front of a huge crowd for the first time in her life and trying not to make any mistakes. The whole experience would be really scary, and anything could go wrong.

She summoned up the same streak of determination that had gotten her through losing twenty-five pounds, and she decided she could handle the situation. Nobody ever got anywhere without a few risks and a lot of effort.

She read through the rules one more time, and filled out her name and phone number. Once she finished, she felt a wave of excitement wash over her.

If she were a cheerleader, people would have a chance to get to know her at last. There'd be no more shyness or self-consciousness over being chubby. After all, she could almost be called slender now. She imagined how she'd look in a red and gold cheerleader uniform. Yes, the effort to win at the tryouts was going to be worth it.

* * *

After dropping off the application, Dee walked through the gym on her way outside to her bicycle. A few girls in white shorts and shirts were standing in a group near the bleachers. Dee knew that basketball intramural games were going on now. The girls must be part of a team that had just finished playing.

As she headed to the door, one of the girls called her name. With her tennis shoes squeaking against the wooden floor, Gloria came running toward her.

"Hi, Dee!" she said with a friendly smile. "What are you doing here so late after school?"

"I just filled out an application for the cheerleader tryouts."

"Good for you!"

"I'm really excited about it."

"You'll have a good chance of being chosen, if what I've heard about some of the other candidates is true. Most of them aren't cheerleader material."

"Who? Do you know any of them?"

"Oh, you know. People like Janice Hofstedder and Marion Whitman." Gloria snickered as she said the names.

"I don't think I know them."

"Neither of them is terribly attractive, so I don't think you have to worry. You can easily beat them."

Dee hadn't thought of trying out for cheerleader as "beating" anybody. All she'd wanted to do was try and win on her own merits. Still, what

Gloria said made her feel she was in with a chance.

"Do you need any help getting your cheer ready?" Gloria asked. "I'd be glad to watch you sometime."

"That's really nice of you Gloria," Dee said. "Right now I've got to think about how I'm going to do everything. But maybe in a few days."

"Well, remember that I'll be glad to help."

"Thanks."

Dee started toward the door again, but Gloria put her hand on Dee's arm to stop her.

"Maybe we could have a Coke at the sub shop some afternoon this week," Gloria said.

"That'd be great, Gloria. But I'll be practicing after school until tryouts. Maybe after that, though."

Gloria looked disappointed, then put a smile on her face. "I'll see you soon," she said and ran back to the group of girls she'd been talking with.

If Dee had time this week, maybe she would ask Gloria to watch her cheer. She could use all the advice she could get. This was something new for her.

When Dee remembered Marc had said Gloria was friends with Jenny, Dee couldn't help wondering what had happened between them. All she knew was what Fiona had told her. Dee wondered if everything really was over between them. Why had Marc gotten so serious when they bumped into Gloria today?

But, then, Dee thought, she had no reason to

pry into Marc's life. Whatever was going on between him and Jenny wasn't her business. Marc wasn't her boyfriend. But Dee knew deep down she was aching to get to know him better. Ever since she'd met him, she'd had a hard time getting the image of those bright blue eyes out of her head.

Chapter
8

Phoebe blinked a few times to adjust her eyes to the dim light of the Little Theater. Woody had asked her to stop by and pick up some of the music he wanted performed at the Arts Fair. She could look it over before their next scheduled practice later in the week, he'd told her at lunch.

As Phoebe walked down the aisle toward the stage, she saw Michael coming toward her in the semidarkness.

"Woody gave me your music, Phoebe," he said. "If you want to, we can go to a rehearsal room and go through it together."

"Okay," Phoebe agreed.

She wondered how Michael was going to act toward her this afternoon. At lunch he'd been almost his usual self. But he hadn't called her yesterday, which was strange. She kept hoping for time alone with him to talk, but they'd been constantly surrounded by other people.

The rehearsal room had spongy accoustical tile on the walls and ceiling and a thick, heavy door that closed behind Phoebe and Michael with a thud. A piano stood against one wall. Several metal music stands and folding chairs cluttered the rest of the small space.

Michael lay the music on top of the piano and took off his green parka.

"We can scream in here if we want to, and nobody'll hear us," he said, glancing at the tile walls.

I feel like screaming, Phoebe thought. Her frustration at not understanding what was going on had been building for two days now. She dreaded having any real problem develop between her and Michael, but at the same time, she couldn't stand not knowing the truth — no matter what it was.

"What's the music Woody chose for the next practice?" she asked and put her backpack down on a folding chair.

"Some songs from *West Side Story.*"

Phoebe gulped. *West Side Story*? That was the musical Griffin was starring in when he fell in love with Sara Carter. Phoebe couldn't possibly stand in front of an audience and sing those songs without choking. She pressed her hand to her forehead and avoided Michael's eyes.

Michael moved closer to her. "What's wrong?" he asked.

"Nothing," she said, massaging her temples.

Michael's face softened with concern. He gathered Phoebe into his arms and held her for a moment.

"I love you, Phoebe," he said. He bent his head toward her and moved his lips lightly over her forehead and nose, finally settling on her mouth for a brief, gentle kiss.

Phoebe couldn't help responding instantly to Michael. The same electricity that had always flowed between them was still there. She loved him more than she'd ever loved anyone. Part of her wanted to snuggle into the warm protection of his arms and forget all she had been thinking about for the past two days.

But the other half was still too confused just to stand there and pretend nothing was wrong. Phoebe wanted Michael to tell her what was happening. It was time for them to get everything out in the open. Yet she didn't want to be pushy about getting him to talk. And she was still scared of what he might have to say.

As if he sensed her conflict, Michael pulled away from her. "I know you've got something on your mind," he said.

"No, *you* do," she answered.

Michael sighed and stood there quietly for a moment. "What do you mean?" he asked.

"You've been so strange since Saturday. I can tell something is wrong."

Michael didn't say anything, and his silence bothered Phoebe more than an angry response would have. "What *is* it, Michael?" she insisted. "What's happening between us?"

Michael sighed heavily again. Finally after a long pause, he looked down at her, his face troubled. "You're right Phoebe. I do have something to tell you. I wish I never had to talk with you about any of this."

"About what?" she asked, alarmed.

"I got a phone call on Saturday from a girl I knew last summer at the music festival."

Phoebe's eyes widened.

"It was before I was with you, Phoebe. It was just for the summer."

Phoebe was sure her heart had stopped. There was a big hollow feeling where it should have been beating. She could feel tears forming in her eyes. "It must have meant something if she's calling you in November. Obviously she hasn't forgotten you."

"She was in D.C. on Saturday. That's why she called." Michael hesitated, as if he were trying to decide what to say next. "She's going to be coming back every weekend to rehearse for a concert, and she knew I lived in the area so she got in touch with me."

"And you'll be seeing her whenever she's here," Phoebe said. She meant it to come out like a question, but a certain finality in her voice made it sound like a foregone conclusion, an inevitability she couldn't fight even if she wanted to.

"Of course not, Phoebe." Michael stood up straighter. "How can you even think I'd rather be with anyone but you?"

"I can think it because you've been acting so weird."

"If I've been weird, it's because I didn't want to have to tell you this. I couldn't decide if I should or not. And then I felt guilty that I hadn't. She's so *un*important to me I figured I didn't need to tell you."

"You mean you'd just start seeing her without even telling me?"

"I don't *want* to see her, Phoebe. You don't understand." Michael shoved his hands into his pockets in exasperation.

"It's all right if you want to be with her," Phoebe said sadly.

"But I don't."

"How can you be sure?"

"I just told you."

"But maybe she's the one you really care about. If you saw her again, it might help you make up your mind."

"I've made up my mind, Phoebe," he said softly, pulling her to him in a tight embrace. He smoothed her curls back from her forehead and kissed her again. They stood that way for a few moments in silence.

"Are you going to see her?" Phoebe asked, pulling back slightly.

Michael stared down at the floor. He sighed, then looked into Phoebe's eyes again.

"I made plans to see her on Saturday."

Phoebe's hands turned to ice.

"I just thought I should. I couldn't very well tell her about you on the phone. I didn't want to hurt her any more than I would want to hurt you."

Even though he meant well, his words stung Phoebe. Of course Michael would want to tell her in person. He was so considerate. But that didn't keep Phoebe from feeling jealous and scared. "What if she tries to persuade you to go back with her? What will you say?"

"I'll tell her there's no point in talking about it. You're the one I love, and that's the end of it."

Now Phoebe looked at the floor. She couldn't get herself to keep her face turned up to Michael's. Not when she felt so confused and unsure.

When he sees her, his feelings might change no matter what he says now, Phoebe thought. Michael's no different from Griffin. It'll be different when he sees her, and he'll want to go back to her. This is all so familiar I can't stand it. Is this going to happen to me over and over, every time I fall in love?

She glanced back up at Michael. His eyes had such earnestness in them, as if he really meant what he had said. But how could Phoebe trust him? Even if he did think he loved only her, just as Griffin once had, she knew everything could change so quickly. She wished she could believe Michael, but deep down she was sure something terrible was on the verge of happening.

"Phoebe," Michael said, cupping his hand under her chin and drawing her face up toward his again. "I love you. Please believe me. I didn't tell you about this right away because I wanted to protect you, that's all. I was afraid you'd think I'd leave you like Griffin did."

Phoebe felt another current of emotion race through her. "I wish I could believe you, Michael. But I can't be sure about anything right now," she said, feeling numb.

"What can I do to make you be sure about me?"

"Nothing. Everything just has to take its course. You have to go meet her. I have to wait and see what's going to happen."

"But nothing will happen."

"It's not that easy, Michael. You don't know how you'll feel when you see her."

"I think I'd better go," she said. With that, Phoebe gathered her coat and backpack and walked out of the practice room.

"But, Phoebe. . . ." Michael called after her. He stuck his head out the door and watched, feeling helpless, as she ran to the end of the hall and went outside.

Chapter
9

Dee shivered in spite of her heavy blue sweat suit and the fluffy mohair muffler she had on. Leaping and jumping as she practiced her cheer didn't ward off the cold much either. Her breath made tiny cloud-like wisps in the chilly air every time she exhaled.

The cheerleading book she'd checked out from the library lay open on the wooden picnic table beside her. She'd finally figured out the three parts of her yell, and she thought she had the whole thing down pretty well.

Dee had always thought cheerleading was simple. It had looked so easy when she'd watched cheerleaders at games and when she'd seen them again last week, practicing after school. But now she knew she'd been wrong. Trying out was going to be a lot more complicated than she'd imagined when she'd signed up last week.

She and Laurie had practiced together a couple of afternoons. Laurie thought that showing their jumps to each other would help both of them. And Gloria had come through and helped her for an hour on Thursday. But even with all the practice, Dee still felt she needed more work.

She went through the routine slowly one more time, making sure she had each move just right. At last, she began to warm up and feel more natural and limber.

Thank goodness she'd been going to her dancercise class the past few months, she thought. If Ms. Welsh hadn't put her through all those workouts, Dee would have been panting for breath by the end of her first yell.

She started practicing the side-arch jump and leapt in the air as high as she could, throwing her arms and legs behind her. Not so good, she thought as she came back to the ground with a slight stumble.

She tried again. This time her jump was higher, and she had more time to get her arms and legs farther back.

Dee jumped again. And again. And again. Her arms began to ache. Finally, she sat down at the picnic table to rest.

She breathed into her cupped hands to keep them warm and stared off into the distance, trying to imagine what Monday's tryouts would be like. She'd run out on stage and start up her cheer. The judges would be sitting there on the front row of folding chairs with pencils and papers ready to evaluate each of her moves. Behind them

64

would be a sea of faces. She'd spot Marc. He'd smile at her, and just seeing him there would give her all the courage she'd need to go through her yell and do a perfect side arch jump at the end. The voice of Dee's mother broke into her reverie.

"Dee, there's someone on the phone for you."

"Who is it?" Her little brother, Billy, peeked out behind her mother.

"None of your business, Billy," Mrs. Patterson answered. "And anyway he didn't say his name."

"It's a boy!" Billy giggled. "Dee's got a boy-friend."

Dee tore up the steps and into the house. Maybe it was Marc. She rushed upstairs to the privacy of the phone in her own room.

When the voice on the other end turned out to be Woody's, Dee sat down on her bed, feeling slightly disappointed. She reached over and picked up her giant panda bear for comfort. She put it in her lap and rested her chin on top of its head.

"I was talking to Jeremy yesterday. He told me you are a fantastic photographer," Woody said.

"That's good to hear."

"Jeremy said you've been doing it as long as he has."

"A few years."

"I thought you just painted."

"No. I do both, but I like photography best."

"Well, that's why I'm calling. You heard us talking about rehearsing for the Arts Fair last Saturday, didn't you?" he asked.

"Sure. Phoebe was worried because Michael missed practice."

"Right. The music is going great. Now I'm trying to find people to donate art for the auction. Do you have anything you could give us?"

Dee thought for a moment. "I have some nice photos of cherry blossoms. And a few from a circus Dad took me to. And they're already mounted on white mats."

"If you're willing to donate them, it would be great. We're trying to raise money for some lighting equipment for the theater and for some printmaking equipment for the art department."

"Wow, sounds like you need to raise a lot of money."

"I have this feeling the Arts Fair is going to be a huge success. This is the first year we're selling student-made objects. If you'll be home, later this afternoon I'll stop by and pick up your photos."

"Sure, I'll be home. Come by anytime."

Dee went back outside to wait for Woody and practice a few more jumps.

Chapter
10

"I'm surprised so many students from the University of Virginia got into the orchestra," Michael said to Leah, their shoulders brushing occasionally as they walked along the sidewalk.

The Lincoln Memorial loomed ahead of them, enormous and imposing with its classical columns and pristine white marble. Leah had suggested they go there for a short walk after lunch.

A whole group of her orchestra colleagues had descended on her and Michael in the concert hall's cafeteria. They'd eaten lunch with so many people that they'd never had the chance to talk. Michael knew that now would be his only opportunity to tell Leah about Phoebe.

"I'm so glad you came to the rehearsal," Leah said, her brown eyes shining as she gazed at Michael. Her soft, full lips turned up into an impish smile. "You can't imagine how much I've missed you."

"I thought you'd have a boyfriend at school by now," Michael said.

"I really haven't met anybody I like as much as you."

"Leah. . . ." Michael started, but something stopped him. The time and place still didn't seem right. Tourists clamored around them, talking in foreign languages and taking pictures. The place was too public, too busy for a personal talk.

Michael looked for a bench where he and Leah could sit far away from the crowd. But he couldn't find one. They kept walking.

Leah brushed a dark curl off her forehead, then pulled her red cape close around her. She moved her hand through a slit in its side and took Michael's arm. Before Michael realized what was happening, she cuddled up close to him.

I've got to tell her now, he thought to himself, his eyes still searching for a more private spot. If he didn't say something soon she was sure to get the wrong idea. He moved his body a few inches away from her for physical and emotional distance. "What did you think of Maestro Van Hauten?" he asked.

"He was extraordinary!"

"I thought so, too."

"What a difference it makes to be playing under someone so talented. I'm amazed at how well he knows every single piece of music."

"The Handel is going to be great."

"I just hope the rehearsing goes this well for the next month." She moved closer to Michael again as they started up the steps into the Lincoln Memorial.

"Don't you wish we were still at the music festival? I never enjoyed anything so much as those three weeks."

Michael nodded. He could tell that Leah was pushing their conversation again toward the closeness they were supposed to be sharing. Leah stopped suddenly on the steps and turned to Michael. "I forgot to ask you, would you like to go to a party at my brother's apartment tonight? He and his roommates are having a big celebration after the Georgetown football game."

"I have to get back by six o'clock." Michael thought of dinner at his house that night and hoped Phoebe would stay after her lesson. "Thank you for asking, though."

Leah's face fell. "I was hoping we'd have some time together. I have so many things I've been saving to tell you."

"I have some things to tell you, too," Michael said.

"You do?" Leah asked, her eyes brightening.

"Yes," Michael answered.

"We don't have much time. I have to head back to rehearsal in a few minutes."

A twinge of panic came over Michael. He had to tell Leah about Phoebe, and he had to do it now. They didn't have all afternoon for small talk.

Michael glanced up at the huge statue of Abraham Lincoln, high above them in a chair, his hands resting on its arms. Honest Abe.

Michael swallowed hard. He'd have to do what he'd come here to do. He had to be as honest — even if it meant hurting Leah.

Michael started to tell Leah about Phoebe, but before he could get out one word, she reached her arms out from under her cape and wrapped them around Michael's shoulders. As quickly as she leaned against him, her lips met with his. Though the kiss was hurried, it was enough to make Michael more uneasy than he'd been all day.

"Oh, Michael, I've wanted to do that since this morning," Leah said, her lips forming the words softly against his cheek. "The minute I saw you I knew nothing had changed between us."

Michael put both his hands on her shoulders and gently pushed her back from him far enough to look her squarely in the eyes.

"Leah," he said, "I have to tell you something."

Michael took her hand and led her quickly down the steps away from Lincoln and the crowds of tourists. All he could think of was how badly he wanted to get this task over with. But viewing this talk with Leah as a task wasn't really right. She deserved better than that. He had cared for her a lot during the few short weeks at music camp.

"Here," he said and leading her to a bench, Leah sat down, too closely, beside him.

"I'm going out with someone else now, Leah." The words settled between them like a concrete wall. "She's very important to me."

Leah pulled back. "You can't just forget about us, Michael. Everything was so wonderful last summer. You couldn't have what we had with someone else."

"You're right. I don't have what we had. I have something different. And it makes me very happy. I'm in love with her." Michael sighed and looked down at his lap. "I don't want there to be any bad feelings between us, Leah. I didn't want to hurt you."

"Oh, Michael, do you really care for her more than you do for me?"

"I've known her for a long time. . . ." Michael began.

"You were together before you met me last summer?" Leah interrupted. "And you didn't tell me?"

"No, Leah. We went to the prom together last spring, but that was all. She was in love with someone else. I didn't have any reason to tell you about her."

"But you loved her all along?"

Michael's breath came out long and heavy. "I guess maybe I did. But I wasn't going out with her."

Leah's brown eyes flashed at him. "I can't believe you were in love with her and still pretended you cared about me."

"But I *did* care about you," Michael protested. His shoulders drooped wearily. "I never lied to you last summer; I enjoyed every minute we spent together. It's just that I'm with someone else now."

Leah looked off into the distance without saying anything, but Michael could tell from the sadness in her face that he had hurt her. Her dark hair waved so beautifully over the red wool of her cape. If he could have done it without hurting her, he'd have touched her hair and comforted her. There was nothing he could do now but wait for her to speak and hope somehow they could still be friends.

She stood up suddenly and turned to face him. Tears were gathering in the corners of her eyes.

"I guess that's it then, Michael. Good-bye."

With a sweep of her cape, she turned back toward the concert hall and walked away.

Michael leaned back against the bench and watched her go. He hated the idea that she would go into rehearsal, upset and unhappy, because of him. Their relationship had been too good, too close to end without them still being friends.

Love was incredibly complicated, he thought, watching Leah disappear beyond a crowd of people getting off a tour bus in the distance. The twists of romance were so strange.

Leah cared about him. He cared about Phoebe. After getting together with Phoebe, he couldn't possibly go back to Leah, even though he had cared for her once.

Love wasn't like that. He knew he couldn't exchange one girl friend for another, like trading baseball cards in grade school. Nobody would ever replace Phoebe. He didn't think he'd ever love anybody as much.

But why had she been so distant from him all week? Whenever he'd called her or tried to talk to her at school, she'd been so guarded. And nothing he said to her seemed to make a difference. Griffin had really hurt her, Michael knew. And now Michael wasn't sure he'd ever be able to make her believe how much he loved her.

Chapter
11

Dee stood at the closet door, rummaging through the dresses and pants and tops that hung in two neat rows. She had thought she would just wear jeans to the tryouts, but yesterday she had realized that jeans would be too tight to move freely.

Now Dee searched through her clothes. Her blue running suit was too baggy. It made her look as if she still had lumps she knew she'd lost three months ago. She picked out a gold and white striped T-shirt, then opened her dresser drawer and took out a pair of white running shorts with a gold stripe down the side. That should do it.

Dee quickly put them on and jumped around a little bit. She could move easily. She stood still and looked at herself in the full-length mirror. In the past week she'd lost three pounds from being so strict with her diet. She hadn't even eaten her usual banana at lunch. And now she had just seven pounds to go. Did those seven pounds still show? Did she look pudgy? Dee eyed her figure in the mirror again.

Maybe her thighs could use an extra inch or so of slimming. But they looked good. In fact, her whole body looked just fine. Nobody could call her chubby anymore.

Dee smiled at her reflection. All those weeks of discipline had been completely worth it. She wouldn't trade anything for the way she felt right now. But even with her excitement, the thought of hundreds of people watching her was really scary. Being the center of attention in front of a huge crowd would be hard no matter what she looked like. The more she thought about it, the more she felt as if a whole flock of butterflies were swooping around in her stomach.

Dee sat down on her bed. Maybe she never should have volunteered to try out. Maybe she'd made a terrible mistake.

But she was already on the list, she couldn't back out now. Sasha had printed the names of all the candidates on the front page of *The Red and the Gold* last Friday. Everyone in the whole school had seen them. If Dee dropped out now, people would know she'd lost courage.

She imagined herself on stage with a gym full of people looking at her. What if she forgot the words of the cheer? What if she stumbled?

"No," she said out loud with a determined toss of her head. The tryouts would go fine. She had as good a chance as anyone. Even if she were hesitant now, she knew she wanted to try out more than anything.

From the wings of the stage, Dee couldn't see how many people had shown up for the tryouts, but judging by the noise they made, she was sure at least half the school was there.

Staying calm wasn't easy with all the candidates milling around, nervously pacing back and forth, and doing knee bends and arm exercises to keep their bodies limber. A tense kind of excitement crackled in the air and there was a sense of impatient waiting. Every minute seemed to crawl by.

Dee saw Laurie standing off by herself and went over to say hello. She hadn't seen her since they'd practiced together last week.

"Have you been working on your side arch?" Laurie asked, her hand smoothing the bell-shaped sleeves of her pink T-shirt in a nervous gesture.

"I practiced all weekend," Dee answered.

"I got Pam Singleton to help me after I saw you. She showed me how to jump a little higher."

As Dee bent down and touched her toes a few times to stretch her muscles, Laurie tried uselessly to peer out at the audience from the stage wing.

"I wish I could see Dick," she said. "He's supposed to be right behind the judges. He said he was going to run to the gym as fast as he could at three-thirty and save a bunch of seats for the crowd."

Dee felt the butterflies start beating their wings

against her stomach again. Marc would probably be right there with them. Dee might be able to see him from the stage. All her excitement came rushing back. She felt the now-familiar, tingly sensation she got whenever she thought of Marc.

The microphone on stage made a few metallic squawks as Ms. Schmidt adjusted it to her height. After she introduced the judges, the regular cheerleaders rushed out on stage in their red and gold uniforms and led a few cheers to get everyone warmed up for the candidates. Dee watched them, wondering if her own motions would look as smooth and effortless as theirs.

Then, one by one, the candidates went out and had their turns. Dee heard the yelling from the gym and knew her moment on stage was getting closer.

"And now," Ms. Schmidt announced at the microphone, "our next candidate is Laurie Bennington."

"Good luck, Laurie," Dee said as Laurie ran out on stage.

The thunder of clapping and shouting that welcomed her told Dee that Laurie was the most popular candidate so far. No one else had gotten such a response even after their cheer, much less before it.

Laurie went through her routine smoothly and confidently. When she did her final pose, the shouting and applause grew even louder.

When Ms. Schmidt announced Dee's name over the loud speaker, Dee's stomach took a nose dive. With every bit of determination she could muster, she made herself walk out on stage. Stiff and frozen, she stood there for a moment and looked at the gym full of faces, which looked to her like a giant blur.

She'd known hundreds of people would be there, and she had tried to imagine how she'd feel with everyone watching her, but nothing she'd imagined matched the reality.

"Okay," she meant to speak normally into the microphone, but realized her voice was so weak that the words came out just above a whisper. She cleared her throat and tried again.

"I'm going to do the yell 'Defeat,'" she managed to say. The audience's enthusiasm was so strong she momentarily forgot her fears.

Walking to center stage, she looked out at the crowd and smiled. Just as she was about to start, she spotted Marc and Fiona waving at her. Seeing her friends gave her renewed courage.

Once she started, she got so caught up in doing her moves she had no time to think of being scared. She went through her routine step-by-step exactly as she had planned it.

Finally, it was time for the side-arch jump. Dee knew she could do it. In fact, she knew she could do it so well that she could hardly wait to get on with it.

She leapt into the air and flung her arms and legs behind her as she'd done so many times before. She felt like soaring. This was her moment. Everyone in the gym was cheering with her. She could feel their energy coming toward her in waves.

But then, suddenly, in the split second she came from her jump back down toward the stage floor, she realized she was off balance. She landed on both feet, then felt her left ankle turn under her as she collapsed in a heap on the floor.

The pain shooting through her ankle and up her leg was nothing compared to the horror of lying there on the stage, awkward and humiliated, in front of so many people. A few students in the audience started to snicker, but most of them sat there in stunned silence. Dee knew they were shocked at witnessing her clumsiness and embarrassment.

As a buzz of whispers and talking filled the gym, Coach Howard, the soccer coach, and Ms. Schmidt hurried on stage toward Dee. They put their arms around her and helped her stand. When she hobbled off with them supporting her, she heard a halfhearted round of clapping follow her. It was that kind of disappointed, embarrassed applause that actors expect after a play that bombs.

As Dee limped off stage, her last thought was that her face might be permanently red.

Chapter
12

"In just a few days, everyone in school will have forgotten your fall," Coach Howard said as he wound an elastic bandage around Dee's ankle. "You'll see. You may feel embarrassed about it now, but these things always pass."

Dee looked down at his gray hair as he bent over her ankle. Even if she did feel like going off somewhere and hiding for the rest of her life, she was grateful for his help.

The coach and Ms. Schmidt had led Dee into his office where he'd motioned for her to sit down on his green-cushioned chair. Dusty soccer trophies lined his window sill and covered his desk. A calendar with a picture of hazy blue mountains was stuck with masking tape to his wall.

This had been such a terrible day of opposites, Dee thought, as she watched him bandage her ankle. Since morning she'd felt fear and excitement fighting it out inside her. Now the battle was between complete humiliation and an absolute determination that she wouldn't let herself just roll over and die.

Dee knew it wouldn't be easy to overcome her embarrassment and pretend it didn't bother her when everyone in school would be talking about it. She wished she could just fade away into Coach Howard's office wall.

"It could have happened to anybody," the coach said as he wound the last bit of bandage around Dee's ankle and fastened it in place with a tiny metal clip. "If I had a nickel for every sprain I've bandaged, I'd be a rich man."

"Thanks for your help, Coach," Dee said.

She winced slightly as she heard another round of yelling drift from the gym through the office door. The tryouts must be just about over. She wished she'd never even heard of them.

"You should be able to hobble around pretty well now," the coach said as he sat down in a chair across from Dee. "Do you have a car?"

"No. My mother brought me to school this morning."

"Can she come and get you?"

"I don't think she's home."

"What about your dad?"

"He's out of town on a business trip."

Dee thought of trying to find Fiona to ask for a ride, but remembered her friend had said she'd come to school on her bicycle.

"Let me see if I can find somebody around here who can take you home," Coach Howard said and walked out of his office.

Dee imagined a trip to her house with Ms. Schmidt trying to persuade her that nobody cared when cheerleader candidates fell down in front of crowds. Or maybe Coach Howard would find some other teacher. Even though everyone would mean well, Dee suspected their attempts to talk her out of her misery would make her feel even worse.

She sighed and leaned back in her chair. Her ankle started to throb slightly, then filled with a deep, dull ache she expected she'd feel for at least a week. Sitting around with Lily wouldn't be all bad, Dee tried to convince herself. And maybe she'd be able to stay home for a few days. Then she wouldn't have to face anybody. And maybe by the time she got back to school again, everyone would have forgotten her humiliation.

As Dee stared at the reflection of sunlight on the brass trophies, she thought she heard Marc's voice in the distance. She sat up straight and listened. Falling down in front of half the school was bad enough. But having Marc see her would be even worse.

She heard the voice again. It *was* Marc's. When she looked up and saw him standing in the doorway, Dee wished she could shrink to three inches and crawl inside one of the coach's drawers.

"I understand you know Marc Harrison," Coach Howard said as he followed Marc into the office.

"Yes," Dee nodded. She felt her cheeks grow hot.

"How's the ankle, Dee?" Marc asked, stooping down to look at her bandage.

"It's okay. The coach fixed me up."

"Does it hurt much?" he asked, touching the bandage lightly with his fingertips.

"Some," Dee said, trying to sound braver than she felt. It hurt terribly.

"It's already swollen up," Marc observed.

"I know."

"I want you to go right home and keep your leg elevated," the coach said. "Soak your ankle in hot water for the next couple of days. Then keep an ice pack on it. And always keep it elevated, okay?"

"Okay," Dee promised.

"Marc offered to drive you home and miss a little practice this afternoon," Coach Howard added.

Dee gulped. The whole experience was getting worse by the minute. "I'm sorry to trouble you, Marc," she said.

"No trouble at all. I'm glad to be able to help."

"You'll miss some laps around the field," Coach Howard said to Marc. "Don't be gone too long."

"I won't."

Marc leaned down and helped Dee up, then held her arm steady as she stepped slowly and cautiously onto the foot with the hurt ankle.

"Ow!" she moaned.

"It'll hurt awhile," the coach offered. "Take a couple of aspirin when you get home. And be sure to keep your weight off it."

"I don't know if I can walk."

"Here, Dee. Lean on me." Marc put his arm around her to steady her and helped her on with her coat. He picked up her backpack and her clothes and led her out to his car.

"Why so quiet?" Marc asked after they'd driven a little way.

"I'm a little embarrassed," she admitted.

Marc looked at her sympathetically. "You looked great out there, Dee. Falling wasn't so bad."

"Yes, it was."

"I've seen cheerleaders fall down lots of times. Just last year before you moved here, John Fisher dropped Carol Morino out on the football field. Both of them ended up on the ground and he was on crutches for a month."

"I know these things happen," Dee said with resignation. "I just wish it hadn't happened to me, that's all."

"I wish it hadn't, too. But you'll be okay. Everybody will probably forget about it before the swelling goes down."

Marc looked over at her and smiled. Dee smiled back. She knew he was trying to cheer her up, and she appreciated his effort. She appreciated even more that Marc didn't seem to think she was so hopelessly clumsy.

But it was hard to believe that everyone would forget about her accident so soon. Though she knew she wasn't ruined for life, she still had weeks of embarrassment ahead of her, people looking at her with pity or amusement, her fall always at the back of their minds.

"Don't get out yet," Marc said, as he stopped in front of Dee's house. "I'll come around and help you."

Marc came around to the passenger side and opened Dee's door. Then with one arm around her shoulders and the other under her right elbow, he carefully guided her out of the car. She steadied herself, and together they walked slowly up the sidewalk to the front door.

Dee had the same feeling she'd had when she sat close beside Marc in Ted's car a week ago. She felt light-headed and giddy, and almost completely forgot about the pain in her ankle. She liked the feel of Marc's strong arm across her back, and the warmth emanating from his body in the crisp autumn air.

He helped her into the family room as if she were a fragile glass sculpture, then settled her back on the sofa and propped her foot up on a pile of pillows.

"There," he said, looking down at her. "You should stay like that until someone gets home."

As he stood up and glanced at the wall across the room, his eyes widened. "Wow! Who made all those model airplanes?"

"My dad. He's an airline executive."

"Does he fly, too?"

"All the time. He belongs to a flying club here."

"I've never seen so many models." Marc walked over to the wall of shelves and looked

85

at the airplanes lined up in neat rows as if they were about to take off down a runway.

"My mom hates them." Dee laughed. "She says all they do is collect dust."

Marc ran his fingers over a tiny DC-6. "This one passes white glove inspection. Is your dad still making them?"

"Now and then, but not so much as before. Mom says he's finally grown up and let Billy take over as the household kid."

"Billy's your brother?"

Dee nodded. "He's eight."

"I've got two brothers. Both older than I am. In college."

"Sometimes I wish Billy were away at school."

"Yeah." Marc gave Dee a knowing look, and they both laughed.

"Billy's not so bad. I shouldn't complain."

"Where is he now?"

"Probably at his dreaded piano lesson."

"I used to hate piano lessons, too. My parents forced me to take them years ago." Marc walked back toward Dee. "So do you have an ice pack?"

"There's one in the bathroom in the cabinet under the sink. It's through that hallway, next to the kitchen."

"Do you want me to bring you a Coke or anything?"

"I'd love a diet Pepsi. They're in the refrigerator door."

Marc headed toward the bathroom.

"Marc?" Dee called him back. "You can make yourself a snack if you want. There's always peanut butter and jelly and usually a full cookie jar on the counter."

"Thanks," Marc said, and disappeared.

Dee heard him hunting down the ice pack and opening up ice trays in the kitchen. She was surprised to find she felt so comfortable, and not at all embarrassed. If the tryouts had to be as terrible as they were, at least they had ended with her getting to spend some time with Marc.

Dee moved her foot slightly, and flinched from the pain.

"Here you go." Marc returned, carrying a tray from the kitchen. He had taken a flower out of a vase in the kitchen and laid it on a napkin on the tray. "An ice pack and a Pepsi for the lady," he said, with an exaggerated flourish. Dee felt her face flush. He gently laid the pack on her ankle. He'd wrapped it in dish towels to keep it from being wet and cold against her skin. When his hands brushed against her bare foot, her skin tingled.

After handing her the diet Pepsi, he sat down on the chair next to the sofa and leaned toward her as he started in on the sandwich he'd made.

"It's nice playing hooky from soccer practice for a while," Marc said.

"You'd be out running up and down the field by now."

"Probably."

"The coach seems like a really nice guy."

"He is. He recruited me for the team, out of one of his PE classes when I was a freshman. I've learned a lot playing soccer."

"Like what?"

"How to work with a group, how to stay in good shape, discipline. I didn't play any sports in junior high." Marc paused. "Coach Howard's approach to soccer is a little like drill camp in the army."

"Sounds great. I'm glad my PE class isn't like that," Dee said.

"I remember." Marc laughed. "Finger push ups. Wrist and ankle exercises." He reached over and squeezed her hand.

Dee grinned at him. "But no ankle exercises for me for awhile."

"I'll bet you'll be doing them in two weeks."

"I hope so."

Marc took his last bite of sandwich and finished his milk.

"I've got to get going," he said and stood up. "If I'm too late for practice, the coach will know I'm staying away and enjoying myself."

Dee smiled at him and their eyes met. Then, quickly, he bent down and brushed his lips over hers. It was so quick, Dee wasn't sure it had happened. And yet the warmth of her lips told her it had.

"Take care of yourself, Dee," Marc said.

"Thanks for bringing me home."

"Thanks for the sandwich. If you miss any school, I can get your assignments for you."

"Thanks."

Dee watched Marc put on his letter jacket and walk toward the front door. As his hand reached the knob, he turned back toward her.

"Would you like to go to a movie Friday night, if you're feeling okay by then?" he asked.

"That would be great!"

"Think you can walk down the aisle of a movie theater?" Marc's blue eyes twinkled.

"Of course."

He turned toward the door again. "I'll call you Thursday night if I don't see you at school before then, and we can decide what to see."

"Okay!" Dee said. "Thanks again, Marc. It was really nice of you to drive me home."

After Marc left, Dee relaxed back against the sofa pillows. She couldn't stop smiling. It was pretty funny that such a disaster had ended up so splendidly. She was going on a date with Marc Harrison, the cutest junior at Kennedy High. She couldn't think of a thing that would make her any happier.

Chapter
13

"Tell me, Laurie," Sasha asked, looking up from her reporter's notebook, "How did it feel when you found out this morning that you'd been chosen cheerleader?"

Laurie sat opposite Sasha in *The Red and the Gold* office on Friday afternoon.

"It was incredibly exciting. I was thrilled. When Ms. Schmidt told me that I'd made it, I could hardly believe it."

Sasha scribbled down Laurie's words in her notebook and continued to ask her questions. When the interview was over, she pulled a plastic bag from her desk drawer.

"Want some trail mix?" she offered. "It'll give you energy for your first cheerleading practice."

"Thanks." Laurie took a handful of the dried fruit and nuts. "I guess I'd better get going."

"See you later," Sasha said. "Your interview

will be on the front page of next week's paper."

Laurie beamed at Sasha as she stood up to go. "Thanks, Sasha."

As she was leaving, Woody walked through the door. "Congrats, Laurie," he called to her as she passed him on her way out. "Hi, Sash," Woody said. He immediately went for the bag of trail mix and stuck his hand inside. "Don't mind if I do."

When he put a giant handful into his mouth and started chomping, his cheeks stuck out like a chipmunk's.

Sasha laughed. "I'd like to put a picture of you looking like that on the front page of *The Red and the Gold* one of these days."

Woody swallowed and reached for more. "This is great stuff."

"It's good for you," Sasha said. "A whole lot better than candy bars."

"But the joy in a Mars bar," Woody countered, "you can't beat that."

Sasha wrinkled up her face in disgust. "Ugh!"

"No offense, Sash," Woody kidded. "Trail Mix is A-okay."

Woody lay a bulging envelope on Sash's desk and sat down in the chair where Laurie had been.

"Were you surprised that Laurie was picked as the new cheerleader?" he asked.

"Not at all. She did so well at the tryouts. I think it's great."

"I know what you mean," Woody agreed. "Since all that trouble over the student government elections last year, it's good she has something new to be involved in at school."

"I think she'll make a better cheerleader than she would have student body president."

"True. But it's amazing how much nicer she's gotten since she and Dick got together."

"That election was so bad last year." Sasha shook her head, thinking of all the copies of *The Red and the Gold* that were stolen in the sabotage attempt. "It was probably the worst experience I've had as editor here, except for some run-ins with John Marquette."

"What do you mean, my little foxette?"

"Woody, cut it out. That's not funny."

Woody shoveled another batch of trail mix into his mouth.

"Have you seen Phoebe lately?" he asked between crunches.

"Not since lunch."

"She looks terrible. At rehearsal today she seemed really upset. I'm worried about her."

Sasha looked thoughtfully at the posters on the wall in front of her. "She has seemed unhappy lately," she said.

"And she hasn't worn a Cub Scout shirt in days."

"A sure sign something's wrong," Sasha agreed. "Do you know what it is?"

"I think she's having some trouble with Michael, but she won't tell me what's going on."

"I could call her later this afternoon and see if I can find anything out," Sasha offered. "She's probably going out with Michael tonight."

"I wouldn't be so sure. I saw him in the hall a

few hours ago, and he didn't look exactly blissful either."

Sasha stuck her pencil in the base of her dark braid as if she were trying to think up a solution. "Maybe Chris knows what's wrong," she said.

As she spoke, out of the corner of her eye she noticed someone coming into the office. She turned and saw Marc's tall frame filling the doorway.

"Here are the names of the Leesburg soccer players," Marc said, handing Sasha a slightly wrinkled sheet of paper. "Coach Howard got them from the Leesburg coach."

"Thanks, Marc." Sasha took the paper and glanced over it.

"We've got to smear those guys," Woody said.

"We will," Marc assured him. "Don't worry."

"Has the coach got you all ready with a bunch of sly maneuvers?" Woody asked.

"You bet," Marc said. "The district championship depends on it. Whoever wins next week will probably get to go to the state playoffs.

"Who's covering the game, Sasha?" he asked.

"Jim Allison."

"He's a good reporter," Woody put in.

"I just lost my photographer, though," Sasha said. "He quit yesterday because his grades were slipping. His parents made him drop out so he'd have more time to study."

"Do you have anyone to take his place?" Marc asked.

"Not yet. I'm getting worried about finding someone in time for the game."

Woody gave Sasha a satisfied grin. "I've got just the person for you."

"Who?" Sasha asked.

"Dee Patterson."

"Dee?" Sasha looked surprised. "Is Dee a photographer?"

"She's been taking photographs for years," Marc said.

Sasha raised her eyebrows. "I didn't know that."

Woody reached over for the envelope he'd brought into Sasha's office. "Here, I have something to show you," he said as he opened it and lay two photographs on the table between Sasha and Marc. "I brought these over to see if you'd use them in the paper to advertise the Arts Fair. Dee donated them. She took them last spring."

Sasha and Marc leaned over to examine the photographs.

"They're great," Marc said.

"Are they ever," Sasha agreed. "For showing me these, Woody, you earned every bite of trail mix."

Woody grinned at her. "Glad I happened by at the right time."

"It would be great if Dee could cover the game," Sasha said as she picked up one of the photographs and studied it more closely. "I'll call her tonight and ask."

Marc looked over at Sasha. "Dee won't be home tonight," he said. "We're going out."

"Could you give her the message to call me then?"

"Glad to," Marc said. "And I'll tell her how impressed you were with her photographs."

"Thanks, Marc," Sasha said as Marc got up to leave.

"I've got to get back to practice. See you guys later."

As soon as he left, Woody looked at Sasha with a knowing grin.

"Did you know he was going out with Dee?" he asked once Marc was down the hall.

"No, but it looks that way, doesn't it?" Sasha responded. "I'm glad. They're both really nice people. I wonder why we haven't heard about it sooner?"

"Maybe Marc wants to keep it quiet," Woody said. "Peter Lacey told me Jenny Woods is pretty upset about their break-up."

"Let's hope Phoebe and Michael aren't breaking up. It would be really hard on her after what happened with Griffin," Woody said.

"Don't worry about it, Woody. I'm sure they'll get things worked out."

"Let's hope so," Woody said, getting up to leave.

Chapter
14

As AMBUSH appeared on the wide-angle screen in huge red letters, space-age music drifted through the air of the theater in high-tech, electronic squeaks. The opening credits flashed on the screen and Dee and Marc settled back into their seats to watch the movie.

"Have some popcorn," Marc whispered, handing the tub of buttered kernels in Dee's direction. The light from the movie flickered blue, then white on his forehead.

"Thanks," Dee said. She took one tiny handful and wished she weighed ninety pounds so she could chomp down free of guilt. The butter tasted rich and salty on her tongue.

She tried to concentrate on the war between the aliens on the screen, but she was constantly aware of Marc's shoulder touching her shoulder, his arm brushing hers whenever he reached for more popcorn.

When the popcorn was gone, Marc put the tub under his seat and wiped his hands with a napkin. Then he casually reached over and placed his arm gently around Dee's shoulders, pulling her close. A chill ran through her as she leaned her head against his shoulder. She hardly noticed what the green-scaled aliens were doing on the screen. The clever camera angles and photographic tricks that had fascinated her a minute earlier went by almost unnoticed. All she was aware of was the warmth of Marc's arm stretched across her back. Her skin tingled every place his body made contact with hers. She shivered and nestled her head into the curve of his neck. When the movie was over, Marc took hold of Dee's hand and led her out of the theater and down the street to his car. He unlocked the door for her, and just as she was about to get in, he placed his hand under her chin and tilted her head back. Without saying a word, he stroked her cheek with gentle fingers and brought his lips down to meet hers in a soft, lingering kiss. Dee thought she might fly away as she silently climbed into the car.

Marc started the engine and turned to look at her. "Do you want to go get something to eat?"

"Sure."

"How about a pizza?"

"Fine."

"I'm starved."

"You just had a whole tub of popcorn."

"Always room for pizza." Marc grinned at her.

"I can see I'm riding with a pizza freak."

As Marc pulled the car away from the curb and started down the street, Dee looked out the window at the stores they were passing. Steffano's Pizza Parlor was just a block ahead. Assuming Marc would be taking her there, she started searching for a parking place. But Marc never slowed down. He drove straight past Steffano's.

"You're not such a pizza freak after all," Dee teased. "You just missed the pizza parlor."

"I thought we'd forget Steffano's and try somewhere where we can be by ourselves."

"The Pizza Haven?" Dee knew it had just opened. She'd been wanting to go there.

"No," Marc said, his face serious. "I was thinking about driving over to Oak Park."

"Oak Park? So far away?"

"It's not that far. We can look around and find a pizza place there."

"Okay," Dee said, puzzled. There were at least eight pizza places in Rose Hill.

Marc glanced over at her. Something about the look in his eyes made her feel uneasy, but it came and went as quickly as the flash of her camera.

Probably no Kennedy student had ever set foot in an Oak Park pizza parlor, Dee thought. Marc must have some reason for driving so far but she had no idea what it might be.

As Dee studied the gray stitching in the felt visor of Marc's car, she sensed that he was hiding something from her.

She looked at his hand on the steering wheel, the same hand she'd held with such pleasure a few moments before. She remembered his gentle kiss and decided not to let her wondering ruin what so far had been a wonderful evening. She shoved her thoughts to a dark, forgotten corner of her mind and stared out the window.

The Oak Park Pizza Corner was a tiny, intimate place with red-and-white checked table cloths covering the small round tables scattered about the room. The smell of tomatoes and peppers and garlic hung in the air. Dee and Marc huddled together next to a lead-paned window, their mushroom pizza and a flickering candle between them. As they watched people walking along the sidewalk outside, their breaths fogged the window.

"Look at that lady across the street," Marc said.

A portly, elderly woman with a pug nose and dropping cheeks hurried along with a boxer at the end of a leash.

Dee giggled at the sight. "Isn't it funny how people always have dogs that look just like them?"

"They could be twins." Marc laughed.

"Do you have any pets?"

"A black lab named Watson."

"Great name!"

"He's nearly ten now, so he's got some gray around his muzzle."

"I guess you two don't look like twins," Dee teased.

"We've got the same ears."

Dee loved the sparkle in Marc's blue eyes when he laughed. The candle cast warm light on his face and made his clear eyes even brighter.

As he took another slice of pizza, the cheese around the edges stretched out into long strings.

"Here," Dee said. She took a fork and helped him tear his piece from the rest on the plate.

Together they cut all the strings, and finally Marc took a giant bite. But as he pulled the pizza slice away from his mouth, the cheese stretched into long strings again.

Dee giggled. "You look great!"

"The pizza's fighting back," he said, struggling to disengage himself from the cheese.

"I wish I had my camera."

"I'm glad you don't." Marc wiped his mouth with a napkin after he finished his bite. "Hey, I forgot to tell you something."

"Hmmm?"

"You may have a new use for your camera."

"Doing what?"

"I saw Sasha in *The Red and the Gold* office this afternoon and Woody was there showing her your photographs." Marc then explained that the regular staff photographer had just quit. "Anyway, they were both really impressed with your pictures. And so was I."

"Thanks."

"Sasha told me to ask you to call her tomorrow. She wants you to cover the Leesburg game for the paper."

"She does?"

Marc nodded. "I said I'd tell you. You'll do it, won't you?"

"I'd love to!"

"You'll have to take lots of pictures of me," Marc teased. "That's part of the deal."

"I'll take hundreds of them."

"I promise I'll smile at the camera. Show all my teeth and the best side of my face."

When Dee started laughing again, Marc reached over and brushed her hair out of her eyes.

She felt as warm as the candle that glowed between them. An hour later it was burning so low the wick sputtered, and Dee and Marc still sat talking and laughing, the empty pizza plate between them. They reluctantly paid the bill, and got up to go.

On the way home when he wasn't shifting gears, Marc held Dee's hand. She leaned toward him in her bucket seat as they wound their way down the dark streets toward Rose Hill, singing along with the radio.

Marc drove to Dee's street and parked far enough away from her house to keep the light of her front-yard lamp from shining in his car. Then he turned to her and pulled her close, until his lips covered hers, soft and searching.

Dee melted into his kiss. The cold November wind blew outside all around them, but inside she felt the sunny warmth of summer.

Marc pulled gently back from her and looked into her eyes. Then he brushed his lips across her forehead, then her nose, and finally her lips.

With her fingertips, Dee felt the worn leather of his jacket, and underneath it the smooth, hard muscles of his back. She wished just then that time would stop, and hold the two of them together forever, as if they were captured for all time in a photograph.

"I've really enjoyed being with you tonight, Dee," Marc whispered softly, his lips moving gently against her temple. He tightened his arms around her.

"Me, too, Marc. I had a great time."

"Do you want to go out after the Leesburg game next Saturday?"

"Sure." Dee looked up at him and started to smile. As the corners of her mouth turned up, their lips met again in a final good-night kiss.

Hours later the memory of Marc's kisses kept Dee warm as she snuggled under the covers in her bed. The thought of Marc's lips on hers thrilled her so much she couldn't sleep. In her mind, she went over and over the way he'd held her and touched her and smoothed his hands over her hair. It had been a perfect evening.

But then her mind skimmed back over that nagging moment of doubt when Marc had said they were going to Oak Park. Why had he driven right by Steffano's and taken her so far away? Why couldn't she get rid of the thought that he was hiding something? Nobody from Rose Hill ever drove so far just for a pizza. Well, maybe he'd wanted to take her some place special.

Dee lay awake, her mind racing. She couldn't

stop wondering why Marc had taken her all the way to Oak Park. Then a thought occurred to her and Dee began to understand. Marc must not have wanted to be seen with her for some reason. He wasn't hiding something *from* her. He was hiding *her*.

Dee sat straight up in bed and looked around in the darkness. Maybe he was dating someone else and didn't want to bump into her. Or maybe he was embarrassed to be seen with her since she fell down at the tryouts. Dee lay back down and propped her injured ankle on a pillow. No, she thought, Marc must have been afraid they would see Jenny Woods. Maybe he still cared about her and didn't want her to find out he'd had a date with Dee.

But if that was the case why had he asked Dee out again?

Chapter
15

The hot fudge sundae melted in front of Phoebe into a puddle of mud. Just one week earlier she'd have attacked it with enough enthusiasm to finish the whole thing off in three minutes. Today, however, she barely noticed it.

Her eyes moved from the pink-and-white striped walls of the ice cream parlor to the white metal chairs around the room to Woody's eyes, which, she felt, were practically boring holes through her. Phoebe knew he was concerned about her, but she wasn't sure he could help.

"You're not sick are you, Pheeberooni?"

"No, Woody, I'm fine." Phoebe's gaze dropped back to the puddle of hot fudge sauce in her ice cream dish.

"Why are you acting so weird then?"

"I'm not acting weird," she said defensively.

"You've been weird all week, Pheeb." Woody put a hand on Phoebe's arm. "Come on, Phoebe.

I'm worried about you. Tell Uncle Woody what the problem is."

Phoebe smiled a tiny smile. Then she sighed and took a halfhearted swipe at her fudge sauce with her spoon.

"Are you still having problems with Michael?"

"Yes."

"Will you think I'm prying if I ask you what they are?"

Phoebe didn't answer.

"Come on, Phoebe," Woody said, leaning forward and resting his elbows on the edge of the white metal table. "What's going on?"

Phoebe looked across the table at him. For some reason, his concern made her sadness even greater. She felt her insides churning and before she could know what was happening, she felt huge, hot tears sliding down her cheeks and plopping down the front of her turtleneck sweater.

"I'm so embarrassed," she said, wiping her cheeks with her white paper napkin.

"Don't be. It's just me. Your pal, Woody."

"I know." Phoebe tried to smile at him.

"So tell me what Michael's doing to get you so upset."

"I think he's falling in love again with some girl he knew at the music festival last summer."

Woody sat up straighter in his chair. "But that's impossible, Phoebe. I've never seen anyone as much in love as Michael. He's crazy about you."

"Not any more."

"What do you mean 'not any more'?"

"His old girl friend called him when she was in D.C. two weeks ago. He saw her last Saturday." Two more fat tears rolled down Phoebe's cheeks.

"But that doesn't mean he's in love with her."

"He went to meet her, though."

"Do you know why?"

"He said to tell her about me."

"So?" Woody shook his head and folded his arms across his chest. "Clearly you're the one he wants."

"But he's been so strange ever since he saw her. I told him I needed time to think, so he's just called a few times. But he's so quiet and distant. Like he's worried or confused. I can tell he doesn't know how to act with me anymore."

"But he must be upset about how you're acting, too. How can he be the way he usually is, when you're obviously so distraught? The strain must be going both ways."

"I don't know, Woody." Phoebe wiped her cheeks again. "I'm just afraid he's fallen in love with her. Maybe he wants to go back with her, and doesn't know how to tell me."

"I'm sure he would tell you if that were the case. But it's not."

"But maybe he's just not sure. Maybe he's trying to make up his mind and choose between us."

"I'm *sure* that's not it. He's been moping around all week just as much as you have."

"That's just the point. He must be moping because he doesn't know what to do."

106

Woody shook his head. "Well, I think it's pretty obvious what's going on, Pheeb."

"What?"

"You're spooked because you think he's being like Griffin."

Phoebe started to cry so hard she buried her face in her arms.

"But he's not like Griffin. You know that." Woody continued. "He's different. More solid. He knows what he wants. And I can tell you it's you."

Phoebe looked up, and blew her nose on a napkin. "I wish I could believe that."

"Even if you don't, just remember that Griffin came back to you. It wasn't like he left you forever. *You* were the one who chose Michael in the end over Griffin. And don't forget how you couldn't give Michael up when Griffin wanted you back. You know Michael would do the same." Woody paused as if he were making sure his words were sinking into Phoebe's brain. "Michael couldn't stop loving you just because some ex-girl friend showed up in his life again."

Phoebe dabbed at her eyes and tried to force a smile.

"That's the way, Pheeb. You look pretty lousy with your eyes all red. Your face won't crack if you smile."

Phoebe couldn't stop from smiling at him now.

"As long as I'm sure you won't drown in a river of tears," Woody continued, "I'm going to leave you for a minute, and go call Kim. I promised to phone her between one o'clock and one-thirty." He looked at his watch. "She'll be stopping at home to pick up some dishes for her mother. We've got to figure out what time we can go out tonight."

Woody's chair scraped across the tile floor as he pushed back from the table. "Will you be all right for a minute?"

"Sure."

Phoebe watched him walk to the pay phone at the back of the ice cream parlor. She looked back down at her sundae and took a few more bites. She and Michael had been at this very place eating sundaes less than three weeks ago.

The thought of their sitting here so happily made Phoebe feel like crying all over again, but she swallowed her tears. No matter what happened between them, she knew she loved him. She always would.

Phoebe remembered how wonderful he'd been when Griffin had reappeared last summer. She had felt so torn between them for awhile, not knowing what to do. It had been one of the most terrible times in her whole life. Just thinking about it now, in fact, made her freeze up inside — even so many months later.

Phoebe leaned back in her chair and wondered if right now Michael were feeling the same way she had last summer, if he were agonizing about what choice to make and feeling tugged in two directions. He might be as upset as she had been, Phoebe realized. She knew she couldn't wish that much confusion on anyone — especially someone she cared for as deeply as Michael.

No matter what was happening between them now, she had to do whatever she could to keep things from being as bad for Michael as they'd been for her. She couldn't let her existence make him feel guilty or confused. She had to make the situation easier for him if she could. She owed him that much.

"Feeling better?" Woody asked as he sat back down across from her.

"Some," Phoebe answered.

"You've come to your senses, then, and realized how much Michael cares about you."

"No, but I've realized how much I care about him."

"That's a start."

"I've got to explain to him that he doesn't have to feel guilty if he wants to go back to his old girl friend."

"You've got it all wrong, Phoebe. You're still not making sense."

"Yes, I am. To me anyway."

Woody reached into his pocket and put money for the sundaes on the little plastic tray that sat between them on the table.

"I guess I want to make sure he knows he's free to make his choice without feeling as miserable as I did when Griffin came back. He can go to his girl friend if he wants to."

"But *you're* his girl friend," Woody insisted and leaned forward toward her again. "You've got to take some advice from your old Uncle Woody. Go to your voice lesson with Miss Spinelli today, and talk to Michael afterward. Give him a chance to tell you how much he loves you."

"Well. . . ." Phoebe sat silently and thought a minute.

"No arguing, Pheeb. You know I give the best advice in town." He reached over and squeezed her arm. "You've got to have your singing lesson anyway. You can't just ignore the rest of your life because of your love life."

"Okay, Uncle Woody," she said. "I'll go."

Woody grinned at her. "And will you please start wearing cub scout shirts again? They're a real tip-off to the rest of us about the state of your mental health."

Chapter
16

As Dee slowly climbed the hill toward Sasha's house, her ankle throbbed slightly. But the heavy elastic bandage gave enough support to keep it from wobbling or feeling extremely weak.

When Sasha had invited Dee to her house earlier that morning, Dee had decided to walk there instead of asking her mother to drive her. Sasha lived only a few blocks away. And since Dee couldn't go to her dancercise class or ride her bicycle yet, she needed the exercise. She wondered how it would be to see Sasha for the first time since she'd fallen at the tryouts. Like everybody else, Sasha would probably act as if it were no big deal. But Dee still felt slightly embarrassed about what had happened.

A cool wind blew right through her sweater and she hugged herself to keep warm. She hadn't stopped thinking about Marc for one minute since she left him last night. She didn't think she'd ever get tired of thinking about him. She smiled as she thought of his kisses and the sparkle in his bright blue eyes.

In the back of her mind, she still felt the nagging fear that Marc still liked Jenny Woods, but instead of worrying something was wrong, she'd decided to focus on all the good things that had happened last night — the kisses, the closeness, the laughter over shared jokes.

Sasha's mother answered the door and pointed Dee in the direction of Sasha's bedroom. Dee found her new friend sitting on a pile of giant patchwork pillows on the floor, talking on the phone.

Sasha waved and motioned to Dee to come in and sit down.

"Why don't we go to the play first and then the party, Rob?" Sasha said into the phone.

As Sasha listened to Rob's response, Dee looked around the bedroom at Sasha's bookcase, and the globe of the world on her oak desk. Framed awards for excellence in writing hung on the wall across from Dee. She sat down on the floor and leaned back against Sasha's bed, which was covered with a brightly colored patchwork quilt that matched the pillows on the floor.

"If you come at seven, that'll give us plenty of time to get to the play," Sasha said. "Okay. See you later." She hung up the phone.

"That was my boyfriend," she explained to Dee. "He wanted to go to a party some of his friends are having tonight because he only comes home every few weekends. But I'd already gotten tickets to a play. We had to figure out what to do."

Sasha drew up her knees and went on. "I'm glad you could come over, Dee. Did Marc tell you why I wanted to see you?"

"He told me you need someone to cover the soccer game with Leesburg."

"When Woody showed me those fantastic pictures of yours, I knew the job wouldn't be a bit hard for you. We need lots of action shots. The only difficulty is being in the right place at the right time. You have to do a lot of running back and forth along the field to keep up with the players — or else have a telephoto lens if you're not right there near the action."

"I think I can do it."

Sasha noticed Dee's elastic bandage, peeping out from the leg of her jeans. She didn't know if she'd embarrass Dee by mentioning her sprained ankle, but she wanted to make sure Dee would be able to run up and down the field by next Saturday. "How's your ankle? Does it still hurt?"

"Not too much. I walked here today. It's getting stronger."

"Great," Sasha said, then glanced down at her hands in her lap. "I hope you're not still feeling bad about your fall."

"I'm starting to feel less embarrassed about it. It already seems like such a long time ago."

"Well, it could happen to anyone." Sasha

stretched out her legs and leaned back against her bedroom wall. "One time, I tripped over an electric cord at a journalism banquet." She started to giggle. "I had to walk up to the microphone to get the award I'd just won, and my foot got all tangled up in the cord. I ended up sprawled out on the floor."

Dee laughed. "I know just how you felt, I'm sure." She was grateful to Sasha for trying to make her feel better. Dee was sure she'd really enjoy working with her.

"I was thinking before you got here, Dee," Sasha said when their fit of giggling had passed. "If you want to be our regular photographer, the job's yours."

Dee gasped. "You mean to cover things besides the Leesburg game?"

"You'd have to cover *everything*. Sometimes Jeremy submits candid shots but he doesn't often cover events."

"That'd be fantastic."

"It's a lot of work," Sasha cautioned. "You have to attend nearly all the school events. Dances. Plays. Games. Our last photographer's grades slipped so badly he had to quit."

Dee knew she didn't have to worry about grades. Hers were always good. "I'd love to do it, Sasha."

"Well, then, welcome to *The Red and the Gold*." Sasha grinned and reached over to shake hands officially with Dee. "Come on, let's go have lunch at Don Pancho's. My treat. We'll celebrate."

* * *

Not much dinner for me tonight, Dee thought as she took a bite of her burrito. She had had a piece of melon for breakfast, and if she just had a small salad for dinner, she could get through this delicious lunch without gaining any weight.

Classical guitar music floated through the air as Dee and Sasha sat at the end of one of the restaurant's long wooden tables.

Sasha sprinkled a little pepper on the lettuce in her taco. "Marc told me you guys were going out last night," she said. "He seemed pretty excited about it."

Dee raised her eyebrows. "He did?"

"Yeah. You two would make a great couple."

Dee couldn't help wondering if Sasha knew Jenny Woods. "Do you know anything about his old girl friend?" she asked.

"You mean Jenny?"

"Uh-huh."

"I know her slightly, but I don't know what went on between her and Marc."

Dee paused and took a bite of her burrito to get courage for her next question. She had to be ready if the answer were "no." "Do you know if they've broken up for good?" Dee asked.

"I think so. But. . . ."

Before Sasha could finish her sentence, Fiona, Diana, and Jeremy walked up to the table.

"May we join you?" Fiona asked in her polite British way.

"Sure," Sasha said, moving over to make room for them.

115

"You should have been at dancercise today, Dee," Fiona said, unbuttoning her blue down jacket. "Ms. Welsh was a terror. She even picked on *me*. She's never done that before."

Dee laughed. "If she's that bad, I'm not sure I want my ankle to get well enough to go back to class."

"How's the ankle doing?" Jeremy asked.

"It's a lot better. I'm almost walking normally."

"You've got to be careful, Dee," Jeremy said with real concern. "I sprained my ankle once and then started running on it too soon. It hadn't healed well enough, and I hurt it all over again. Rather badly."

"I'll be careful," Dee promised.

"Her ankle's got to be well by next Saturday," Sasha said, smiling. "Dee's the new photographer for *The Red and the Gold*. Her first assignment is the Leesburg soccer game."

"Hey, congratulations." Jeremy gave Dee a pat on the shoulder.

"Thanks," Dee said.

"That's really great, Dee," Diana said.

"And the Leesburg game!" Jeremy said. "What a way to start your new job!"

"I know." Dee took a sip of her diet Pepsi.

"Don't get caught up in any fights on the field," Diana said, remembering her brother Bart's injury during a Leesburg football game. "They're pretty rough players who take their sports really seriously."

"Everybody's already in an uproar about that

game," Jeremy said. "That's all I hear anyone talking about."

As he was speaking, Laurie and Dick came in and sat down at the end of the table. It was the first time Dee had seen Laurie since the tryouts. When they smiled hello to each other, Dee realized she wasn't nearly so embarrassed as she thought she would be. And Dee didn't even feel uncomfortable that Laurie had been chosen cheerleader and she hadn't.

Sasha had told Dee that a year ago, Laurie would never have let her forget what a mess she'd made of the tryouts. But ever since she started going out with Dick Westergard, Laurie had been doing her best to be a little more charitable. Dee was glad she hadn't tried out a year ago.

Laurie had overheard Jeremy's comment and she asked, "What's everyone in an uproar about?"

"About the Leesburg soccer game."

"It should be exciting," Dick said.

Laurie nudged Sasha's elbow. "Here comes Gloria Macmillan," she said in a whisper and nodded in Gloria's direction.

Everyone at the table watched Gloria walk through the restaurant and sit down at a table in the corner. She asked the waiter for two menus, and Dee wondered if Jenny Woods were meeting her there.

"It's not polite to stare," Fiona reminded everyone at the table.

"We're not staring," Laurie said. "Just looking."

"I keep telling Laurie she's got to forget Gloria," Dick said.

"I have," Laurie said a little defensively. "I'm not angry at her anymore. I've talked with her lots of times."

"But you haven't exactly forgiven her," Dick said.

"I'm not going to, either," Laurie said acidly. Then she looked at Dick. "Would you?"

"Well, probably not," he said with a smile.

"What's so bad about Gloria?" Dee asked.

"She's not bad exactly," Laurie said with effort. "But she ruined my campaign for student government last year."

"But look who won instead," Dick teased, referring to his own victory. He put his arm around Laurie and squeezed her shoulders.

When a gray-haired woman came into Don Pancho's and sat down with Gloria, Dee was extremely disappointed. Gloria's grandmother, she thought. When would she ever get to meet Jenny?

Chapter
17

Phoebe pedaled her bicycle close behind Michael's. She always tried to stay near him when they went riding together. Sometimes they coasted along side-by-side, but today she liked the feeling of his leading and her following in his path.

Michael shifted the gears of his bicycle and leaned forward over his handlebars as he pedaled up the incline at the entrance to Rose Hill Park. Over the heavy Irish sweater Phoebe had given him for his birthday, his red windbreaker flapped like a flag in the wind.

With Phoebe following, they passed through the wrought iron gate at the entrance of the park and started riding along the curving road toward the Rose Garden.

What will he think when he hears what I want to say? Phoebe wondered. Will he be glad I've tried to be so understanding? She had no way of knowing. At least not now.

She had no way of knowing. At least not now.

As soon as Woody had dropped her off at home, she'd gone to her bedroom and called Michael. By then she was more determined than ever to talk with him no matter how much courage it took. He simply *had* to know he was free to make his choice between her and Leah. She cared too much about him to stand in his way.

But Michael apparently had no idea what was on her mind.

"We need to talk," Phoebe said, trying to put as much conviction into her voice as possible.

And that was all it took. Michael hung up the phone and speeded over to Phoebe's house in less than five minutes.

As Phoebe pedaled along, she stared ahead at Michael's dark hair tousled by the wind. His shoulders looked so strong and broad beneath his windbreaker. Phoebe always loved seeing him wear the sweater she'd bought him.

Michael slowed down and pulled over toward the curb. He pointed to the Rose Garden in the distance.

"Is over there okay?" he asked, turning back toward her.

"Fine," Phoebe said.

"Let's go." Michael started up again and headed toward the garden. He looked back now and then to make sure Phoebe was behind him. They turned onto a gravel path that led into the

Rose Garden, their tires making crunching noises against the tiny stones.

In the chill of November the rose bushes had become gray, spiked skeletons. Months ago the colorful roses had faded and dropped to the ground. Only a few sodden leaves hung listlessly from the tough green stems. Without the leaves, the thorns seemed more pronounced, their jagged points more scratchy and cruel. Under the gray afternoon sky, what had once been a beautiful garden now gave the feeling of loneliness and desolation.

Michael leaned his bicycle against a metal railing by the path, and Phoebe did the same. They walked side-by-side toward the wooden bench where just a few months earlier they had laughed and talked together in the early autumn sunshine.

When they sat down, the bench felt cold and damp beneath their clothing. Phoebe looked at the tangle of stems and thorns in the rose bushes. Could what Michael might say to her scratch and hurt as much as all those thorns? Yes, she told herself, it could.

Michael put his arm around her and drew her toward him. Gently with his fingertips he tilted her chin up so her mouth was almost touching his. Then he kissed her, softly.

"I love you, Phoebe," he whispered. "No matter what happens between us, you must always remember that I love you."

He leaned closer toward her and kissed her again.

Phoebe kissed him back eagerly, realizing how much she had missed his kisses, his warm laughter, his presence these past few weeks.

Phoebe forced herself to move away from Michael. It took all her determination to start what she had to say.

"Michael," she began, then bit her lips as if she didn't want her words to pass through them.

Michael's brown eyes softened as he looked at her attentively.

"Michael," she started again, then touched her forehead with her hand. "I don't know how to say what I have to say."

"Then just say it however it comes out."

Phoebe cleared her throat and began again. "I want you to know I love you."

Michael smiled at her and ran his hand gently over her red curls. "I'm glad you do," he said.

"But it's not how you think . . . I mean. . . . Well, I *do* love you. . . . This all seems so crazy. . . ."

"What?" Michael interrupted. His shoulders stiffened slightly.

"I mean, I love you too much to want you upset about me. I don't want you to worry about deciding between me and Leah." Phoebe wrung her hands. "If you think she's the right person for you, then that's okay with me."

"I've told you over and over again," Michael insisted, "you're the one who's right for me."

"But I don't think you really mean it. You've been acting differently ever since you saw her."

Phoebe's voice cracked as the words came out. "I wanted to tell you that I won't hate you for going back to her. I think too much of you ever to do that."

"Do you *want* me to go back to Leah?" Michael asked. "Is that what you're trying to say?" The confusion in his voice was too apparent to go unnoticed.

"I just want you to know I'll still be your friend if you do. I want you to be free, that's all."

"Free?"

"To make your choice — without thinking you'll hurt me if you want her."

"You sound like you've made my choice for me," Michael said, his face reddening. "If you've already gotten everything worked out so well, why are you bothering to talk to me?"

"I *don't* have everything worked out." Phoebe felt all her resolve about being calm and loving start to wash away. Michael wasn't understanding the effort she was making for him. He wasn't even trying to see her side.

"What do you think, Phoebe? Do you think I can trade you in for Leah? Just exchange you like taking clothes that don't fit back to the store?"

"No, Michael," Phoebe protested. "I just thought. . . ."

"Have you forgotten how we feel about each other? If you want to break up with me, then do it directly. Don't make it out like I'm the one who wants to do it."

"But. . . ." Phoebe was so shocked by Michael's reaction that she couldn't finish what she started to say.

"If you don't want to be my girl friend, that's just fine with me." Michael jumped to his feet with an angry jerk of his head. "I can manage without you."

He turned his back on Phoebe and walked away, leaving her to feel as if ice water were flowing through her veins instead of blood. I never loved anybody so much in my whole life, she thought. What's happening to us? She held back her tears until she saw Michael climb on his bicycle and ride away.

Then she sat on the bench for a long time, waiting for the numbness to flow out of her enough to get back home. Never, ever would she have expected Michael to react as he had. He was obviously twisting around what she'd said so he could break up with her without being honest about his real reasons. He didn't care about her. He probably never had. All he'd said about loving her forever meant absolutely nothing. Leah had probably always been on his mind.

Chapter
18

A cheer thundered from the soccer stadium. Robert McCallum had scored a goal for Kennedy. He'd kicked the ball past the Leesburg soccer players with a calm, cool efficiency that left them completely unprepared.

"Way to go!"

"Yay, Rob! Do it again!"

Dee looked up from the field where she was standing. Red and gold pom-poms fluttered in a frenzy in the afternoon sun. She felt her skin start to prickle from all the excitement.

All week she'd been preparing for her first assignment for *The Red and the Gold*. On Monday, she studied a book on soccer to learn more about the rules. On Tuesday, she sat high up in the stadium with her telephoto lens and practiced taking the action shots. On Wednesday, she elevated and gently massaged her ankle to strengthen it.

Now with the cheers and shouts and frenzy of the Leesburg game, Dee was so excited that she wouldn't even have noticed any pain in her ankle. She hobbled up and down the sidelines and tried as hard as she could to keep up with the players.

Dee watched Marc especially. He looked so handsome in his soccer uniform. Sweat poured down his ruddy cheeks in spite of the cold November wind.

At halftime the boys ran off the field, and Dee went to sit on a bench and rest for a minute. In the distance she watched the Kennedy cheerleaders shaking their pom-poms and leaping in the air. If she hadn't fallen down at the tryouts, she wondered, would she be there instead of Laurie?

She leaned back against the wooden bench and smiled. Maybe she would have been chosen. She'd never know for sure. But whether or not she was a cheerleader didn't matter now. If felt so good to be sitting right there on the soccer field, knowing that she'd rather be doing exactly what she was doing than anything else she could imagine. She was grateful things had turned out this way.

Dee had just finished loading another roll of film into her camera when the soccer team ran onto the field again. Marc looked over at Dee and waved happily toward her. She grinned at him. Soon she was running up and down the field again, shooting photographs as quickly as she could.

* * *

The game was a battle of endurance and skill. Both teams seemed equally matched. With just a few minutes left in the game, the score was tied at two goals each.

We've *got* to win, Dee thought as she rushed back toward the Leesburg goal. "Come on!" she shouted as she wound the film on her camera to the next frame.

With only two minutes left, the score was still tied, and the shouts that filled the stadium were so loud they hurt Dee's ears. The Leesburg team had the ball and they were headed down the field toward their goal.

A Leesburg player kicked the ball with such speed and force it made a smacking sound. The Kennedy defense frantically chased the Leesburg forward who had received the pass, trying to get the ball away. Just as it looked as if he would take the ball all the way down the field to make the goal, Marc lunged ahead of him, intercepted the ball, and knocked it to a Kennedy player.

Kennedy had the ball! Dee hurried down toward the other end of the field after the Kennedy players, who went by in a streak of red and gold. When they crowded together again, Dee thought maybe Leesburg had gotten the ball back. Enough time was left in the game for them to run down the field again and score.

Dee made her way toward the Leesburg goal. She was determined to get there if her team were going to score. As she got close to the players, she saw Marc get the ball away from the group. He passed it to Rob McCallum, who kicked it back. Dee got her camera ready and stood waiting.

In a flash before her, Marc ran closer to the Leesburg goal. She aimed her camera at him, ready. He raised his leg in a powerful stroke, and Dee clicked her camera just as he plunged the ball with a sure, swift kick past the goalkeeper and across the line for a Kennedy goal.

The roar that went up in the crowd behind Dee was deafening. She looked up in the stands and saw Leesburg students in their blue military uniforms booing angrily.

Dee searched for Marc, but he was engulfed in the crowd that had rushed onto the field. Marc had won the game for Kennedy! And she'd captured his moment of glory on film.

As Dee hurried to pack up her camera equipment, she saw Marc running toward her.

"You won the game!" she yelled at him.

He scooped her up into his arms and gave her a hug that took her breath away.

"We won, Dee! We won!" he shouted, even though they were pressed so tightly together she could have heard him whisper.

"You did it!" Dee hugged him even tighter.

Laughing, Marc swung her around in a circle, then put her down. "I'll see you in a little while," he called back to her as he ran to catch up with the rest of the team heading toward the locker room.

The emotion running through the crowd outside the locker room was almost thick enough to see. Leesburg cadets glowered at the Kennedy students, who were still whooping and shrieking victoriously. Dee had yelled so long and hard her voice was hoarse. Even trying to talk with Fiona above the noise was hard.

"Wasn't that fantastic?! As good as English soccer!" Fiona shouted to Dee. "Marc was great."

As the two girls waited for the Kennedy team to come out of the locker room, the crowd gradually began to thin out. But excitement still flowed through the air like an electric current.

Fiona nudged Dee's arm and leaned toward her to whisper in her ear. "That's Jenny Woods over there by Gloria Macmillan," she said, nodding in their direction.

"The blonde?"

"Yes."

"Do you think Jenny's come to see Marc?" Dee asked, her eyes widening.

"I don't know. . . ." Fiona started to say, but before she could finish her sentence, a rowdy group of Leesburg boys standing near them started shouting and pushing some Kennedy students. The cadets were obviously angry about losing the game and were taking their frustration out on whoever was standing in their way.

Soon the yelling and shoving started spreading through the whole crowd. It looked like a fight was about to break out. Someone standing near Dee got pushed and almost lost his balance. He accidentally knocked his shoulder against hers so hard she nearly fell down.

Fiona grabbed Dee and tried to pull her out

129

of the way before anything more could happen.

"Come on," she said and led Dee by the arm toward the edge of the crowd.

Dee tried to push away from the uproar, but the crowd was so dense she had a hard time getting by the other people. Her heart started to pound.

"Come on," Fiona shouted.

Before Dee knew what was happening, a few more Kennedy boys in the crowd pushed their way toward the Leesburg boys and started yelling at them. As Dee tried frantically to dodge behind them and move out of the way, she was afraid she was going to be caught right in the middle. But then she looked up and saw Marc pushing his way toward her.

"Get out of here," he shouted at the Leesburg boys. Some of his team members were behind him.

Dee and Fiona managed to make their way to the edge of the crowd. They watched, frightened, to see what would happen, and in just a few seconds the shoving and yelling of the Leesburg boys began to escalate into a real brawl.

"What's going on here?" someone shouted from the locker room door. Dee saw Coach Howard, pushing his way toward the boys. "Okay, that's enough. That is enough," he said, pulling two boys apart. "Break it up, everybody. It's time to go home."

At last Marc emerged from the crowd. He practically flew toward Dee, and again he swept her up in his arms and spun her around.

Chapter
19

"Are you all right, Dee?" Marc asked, his eyebrows drawn together with concern.

"I guess so." Having Marc there with his arm around her definitely made her feel safer.

"I was really afraid you were going to get hurt."

"Me, too. That was pretty scary."

As Dee and Marc moved away from the crowd, she glanced back to where Jenny had been standing. She was still there, watching them. She looked as if she were about to cry. But the minute she saw Dee look at her, she turned away.

Dee didn't know whether or not to point her out to Marc. She had no idea what his reaction would be. And right now all the uproar over the Leesburg boys was much more on their minds. Marc looked pretty angry.

Dee brushed her fingertips over the lines on his

forehead. "I've never seen you scowl before," she said.

"Well, that was a horrible scene. Those guys are such poor sports."

"Forget about it now, Marc. At least we won."

"You're right." He smiled.

"And you scored the winning goal."

"I can't believe I managed to get the ball at the end."

"I've never seen anybody take over the way you did."

"I'm glad you were there, Dee," he said, squeezing her hand.

"Me, too. I got some great shots."

"Did you get the last goal?"

"Uh-huh. And if I have any say about it, it'll be on the front page of next week's paper."

"People will think I'm bribing you for publicity." Marc started to laugh, then bent down and gave Dee a quick kiss on the cheek. He gently placed his hand on the back of her neck and pulled her closer.

"Want to go to the sub shop and grab a bite?" he asked.

"Sure."

Dee felt like skipping down the hill. At last Marc was taking her where they'd be seen together. Everyone in the whole crowd would probably be in the sub shop now. Going to Oak Park must just have been an unexplainable whim of Marc's last Friday night. Maybe he hadn't been trying to keep from being seen with her after all.

They parked down the street from the sub shop

and as Dee got out of the car, Marc tugged at her sleeve and said, "I'll beat you to the door."

"Hey, no fair! I'm an injured athlete!" Dee shouted after him.

"Excuses, excuses," he called back.

Marc was leaning against the door to the sub shop when at last she reached him. She was just about to tell him what she thought of a soccer star who would take advantage of a poor, injured, would-have-been cheerleader when he grabbed her and picked her up just as he had on the soccer field. He swung her around in a circle again and again. When he put her down, he kissed her gently. Dee couldn't remember a time in her life when she felt so happy. Arm in arm, they walked through the heavy oak door into the sub shop.

They were greeted by the usual blast of music. Trying to get used to the noise, Dee looked around for friends to sit with. Her eyes went up and down the long tables, but she couldn't find any familiar faces. Then she searched each booth, one by one, around the edges of the room. No one she knew was sitting in any of them.

The eager smile on Dee's face faded.

"Nobody's here," she said without being able to hide her disappointment.

"They've probably all gone over to Peter Lacey's," Marc said. He tilted his head back to read the menu on the sub shop wall, and Dee had the feeling he didn't want to look at her.

"Is Peter having a party?" she asked, trying to act as if she weren't too interested.

"Yes."

"Oh." Dee's lips closed softly around the word.

So she'd been wrong. Marc still didn't want to be seen with her. Or else he was hiding something. Dee could tell from the hardening of his jaw that he was troubled. He must know she suspected something was going on.

"I just didn't feel like going there tonight," Marc said finally. And the subject dropped.

Their shoulders touched slightly as they studied the menu on the wall again. When Marc went to the counter to give their orders, Dee found an empty booth along the wall and sat down to wait for him. She stared blankly at the people sitting across the room. She couldn't imagine why Marc didn't want to be seen with her.

Dee knew how Jenny must have felt, watching Dee walk away with Marc. It couldn't have been easy for Jenny to see someone she cared so much about with another girl. And Dee suspected she might soon be in Jenny's place, wanting someone so badly, and not being able to have him. She dreaded finding out what Marc was hiding.

She sighed. Resting her elbow on the edge of the table, she pressed her fingers to her forehead. Marc brought their food to the booth and slid in across from her. Avoiding Dee's eyes, he took a giant bite of his submarine sandwich and chewed it thoughtfully. "I guess we have to talk," he said, finally. "I can tell you're not too happy, and I want to explain to you what's going on."

Dee was silent. Marc looked straight into her eyes and started to speak. "I didn't want to go to

Peter's party because Jenny Woods is going to be there."

The mention of Jenny's name stung Dee. So he was going to tell her he was dating Jenny, too. Maybe even that he loved her. "Would it be so bad to see her at the party?" Dee asked and braced herself for Marc's answer.

"It wouldn't be too bad for me," he said. "But I was afraid it might be hard on you. And I know it would be hard on Jenny."

Dee remembered the dejected look on Jenny's face.

"Jenny called me last night and tried to get me to go back with her," Marc continued. "She wanted me to meet her at Peter's party."

"Did you want to see her?" Dee asked.

"No. I wanted to be with you."

Dee could tell he meant what he was saying, but she still felt confused — and a little threatened.

"You look upset," Marc said, his bright blue eyes searching her face.

"I just wish I understood what was really going on."

"It's simple, Dee," Marc said. "Jenny and I broke up a month ago. I knew then I'd never go back to her again. But she hasn't accepted it. I was afraid of what might happen if you and I ran into her anywhere. I wasn't sure how you'd feel."

"It would have been okay." Dee paused. "I guess."

"We're just getting to know each other and I didn't want there to be any problems."

"I understand," Dee said. "I just wish everything weren't so complicated."

"It's not complicated. As long as you understand what's going on."

Marc put down his sandwich and reached across the table for Dee's hand. "I really care about you, Dee. I don't want anything to mess up what's happening between us, because I think it's really special."

Dee smiled at him. "I think so, too."

"So finish up your salad and we'll go for a walk," Marc said. "You haven't eaten a bite."

But Dee wasn't really hungry anymore. She felt so relieved and happy she wanted to shout for joy.

When they left the sub shop, she and Marc walked together along the river as the sun went down and the lights of nearby houses twinkled against the flowing water. When they sat down on a stone bench and watched the moon, Marc held her close. They talked as if there would never be enough time to say all they wanted to each other.

At the end of the evening when Marc pulled up in front of Dee's house and gathered her into his arms, she was sure she was in love.

Chapter
20

Dee hurried toward *The Red and the Gold* office on Monday morning. If she got there before eight-thirty, she'd have time to talk to Sasha and let her know the photographs of the Leesburg game would be ready by Wednesday — in plenty of time for the newspaper deadline.

Dee hadn't been able to make the prints on Sunday. Her father had insisted the whole family go to an exhibit at the Smithsonian Institution. They didn't get home until late in the afternoon, and she'd spent the rest of the day doing her homework.

Dee hurried around the corner toward Sasha's office. When she was just a few doors away, she felt a tap on her shoulder. Turning around, she found herself face to face with Gloria Macmillan.

"Dee," Gloria said, a broad smile on her face. "I was hoping I'd find you before class."

"Hi, Gloria. What's up?" Dee asked pleasantly.

"I wanted to talk to you."

Gloria pulled Dee over toward the lockers at the end of the hall. Dee leaned against the cold, hard metal, out of the way of people on their way to class.

"I know you're not going to want to hear this." Gloria bent nearer and whispered as if she and Dee were the closest of friends. "But I thought I should tell you. I wanted to do what I could to help."

Dee gave Gloria a puzzled look. "What do you mean?"

"I wanted to let you know that Marc still likes Jenny."

"What?!" A tiny snap of shock went through Dee's body.

"He's just taking you out to make Jenny jealous."

"But that's impossible."

"It's true," Gloria insisted. "Marc's trying to get her back and I thought you'd want to know."

"How do you know what you're talking about?" Dee demanded.

"Jenny told me. Over the weekend. And Marc said so, too. At first he wanted to get back at Jenny by asking you out. But then when they started talking about getting back together last weekend, he already had the date with you. He didn't take you to Peter Lacey's party because he didn't want Jenny upset seeing him there with you. That might have kept them from getting together."

The image of Gloria and Jenny standing together after the soccer game came to Dee's mind — and the hurt look on Jenny's face. She remembered, too, Marc's saying that it would upset Jenny if she saw them together at Peter's house. She remembered how strange he'd acted the day they bumped into Gloria while they were waiting in line.

"Marc has a date with Jenny tonight," Gloria continued, finally. "They're a couple again."

"That can't be true," Dee insisted. A chill crept slowly down her spine. "You're making it up, Gloria. Marc's not going back to her. He told me."

But maybe it was true. How could Dee know for sure? She'd just met Marc a few weeks ago. All she really knew about him and Jenny was what he'd told her — and then a few second- and third-hand rumors.

"I know this is upsetting, Dee," Gloria said, putting her cold hand on Dee's arm as if to offer comfort. "I didn't want to be the one to tell you. But I thought it would be worse if you were caught by surprise. You shouldn't get hurt any more than you have to."

"Sure, Gloria," Dee whispered. Gloria looked so concerned. For all Dee knew, Gloria could be perfectly right about Marc. But nothing made sense. Or did it?

"If I can help you, Dee, let me know." Gloria patted Dee's arm again and walked away.

"Sure." Dee's voice trailed off into a whisper. Even if she'd had time now, Dee couldn't bring herself to see Sasha. She walked to first-period class in a daze, feeling as if she'd just swallowed poison. She'd have given anything to be home right now. Where she would bury herself under her blankets and hug Lily for comfort. She wanted to be by herself where she'd have time to think and figure out just what was going on.

But now she was at school — alone. And she was going to have to get through this day. She felt tears brimming in her eyes, but she forced them back.

Dee dragged through her morning classes like a weary robot. She sat at her desk and looked at her teachers, but her mind was continuously weighing all that Gloria had said. Gloria could be lying. But she could be telling the truth. What did she have to gain by lying? She had said she wanted to keep Dee from being caught by surprise.

But Dee wouldn't be caught, she told herself during lunch when she hid in the restroom. The next time she saw Marc, she'd act as if everything were fine. If he wanted to go back to Jenny, that was all right. She'd get along. She'd make sure he realized she didn't need him.

And yet she knew she really liked him. More than she wanted to admit. Why had she let herself be so vulnerable? Why had she ever fallen in love?

The three-thirty bell rang, shrill and piercing, but it was like music to Dee. It marked the end of the worst day she'd ever spent at school, and

140

now she was free to go home, to be alone at last.

When she got outside, she found as dark and gloomy a November day as she had ever seen. The sky was gray. A fierce, cold wind whipped around her.

As she headed outside, it started to snow. As the soggy flakes blew against her face, she could hardly tell them from the tears that were sliding down her cheeks.

The sooner she got home, the sooner she could be alone, Dee thought, and started walking faster. As she stepped down from the curb to cross the street, her foot slipped on the icy asphalt. She grimaced. She bent down and wrapped her hand around the pain.

"Are you all right?"

Dee quickly wiped her tears away with the back of her hand and looked up to see Phoebe standing beside her.

"I thought I turned my ankle again, but it's okay."

Phoebe looked at the stain of tears on Dee's face. "Does it hurt that badly?" she asked, slightly alarmed.

"Oh." Dee suddenly realized that Phoebe was referring to her tears. "I'm not crying about my ankle," she said and tried to smile. "It's something else."

If Dee had known Phoebe better, she'd have told her what had happened. Phoebe looked so friendly and yet so unhappy. She'd be a real partner in misery, Dee could tell. But Phoebe was also part of the crowd. She knew Marc. And

Dee didn't feel like she could trust anyone anymore.

"Can you make it home okay?" Phoebe asked.

"I think so. I don't have too far to walk."

"I wish I had my mother's car so I could drive you."

Phoebe's kind words almost made Dee start crying again. "I'll be okay. Thanks, Phoebe."

As Dee got closer to her house, she passed the place where Marc had parked his car on Saturday. The bare branches of a cherry tree blew above it in the wind. Just looking at the spot made Dee flinch. She had been so happy there just two days before.

By the time she got home, she couldn't remember when her house had ever looked so inviting. She hurried in and slammed the door behind her.

Chapter
21

Dee was glad no one was home. Only Lily came to greet her as she walked into the entry hall and hung her parka in the closet. As Dee bent down to pet Lily, the cat rubbed against her leg. The softness of her fur was comforting.

Lily was about the only living thing Dee wanted to see right now. If her mother or father were home, they'd notice something was wrong. If Billy were there, he'd be pestering her to play a game on their computer. She felt like climbing into bed until spring came.

Dee put her books down on the dining room table and walked into the kitchen to fix herself a cup of peppermint tea.

She found a note from her mother on the refrigerator door.

Dee,
I've gone to meet your father for a
party at his office. We'll be home late.
Billy's at cub scouts till 5:00. There's
a casserole in the fridge for you to heat
up for dinner. See you later,

      —Mom

Good, Dee thought. I'll be alone til five o'clock at the least.

She glanced down at the note again and saw a tiny arrow at the bottom of the page. The minute Dee turned to the back, her heart started beating faster.

P.S. Marc called at 3:35. Said he
hadn't seen you at school today and
wondered if you were sick. I told him
you were fine.

Marc had called. He was worried about her. Maybe he really cared.

But then Gloria's words came rushing back to her. He must have been calling to tell her he was going back to Jenny.

Dee was glad she hadn't been there when he'd called. She didn't want to face Marc yet. If he were going to reject her, then she was going to have to be ready for it.

Lost in thought, Dee stood there in the kitchen for a long time, holding her mother's note and staring at the tiles on the kitchen floor. A year was a long time for two people to go together. Marc and Jenny must have had a lot between them after all that time. Even though he'd thought for a while he wanted to break up with Jenny, he had probably discovered that he couldn't give her up after all he'd felt for her for a whole year. Dee could understand that, she guessed. But it hurt too much to think about it. And another part of her didn't understand at all. Marc had seemed so sincere when he'd told her he cared about her. Had he been making it all up?

The phone started to ring, a shrill, harsh ring that jolted Dee out of her thoughts. It might be Marc, Dee thought. Because of the snow, Coach Howard had probably ended practice early today. And Marc might be trying to reach her again.

Dee counted the rings. Five. Six. Seven. Ten rings. She couldn't bring herself to answer.

Dee lay moping on her bed with Lily until Billy came home from cub scouts. They ate a quick dinner together, and Dee returned to her room.

When the phone rang, Billy shouted, "I'll get it."

Dee stuck her head out of her room and screamed, "No!"

"But it might be for me," Billy protested. "And what if it's Mom or Dad?"

"They'll call back," Dee argued as the phone kept ringing. "Please, Billy, don't answer it."

"Why not?"

"Because there's someone I don't want to talk to."

"That's crazy. I'm answering it."

145

But by the time he got there, it stopped ringing.

When Billy was settled back in front of the television set in the family room, Dee emerged from her room and went to the darkroom her father had built right after they'd moved to Rose Hill.

The room was a private haven for Dee, a secret place where no one else in the family ever went. Only Lily was invited in occasionally.

Two long tables stood against the walls, surrounded by shelves of developing solutions and trays and an enlarger, which her father had miraculously found for only fifty dollars at a garage sale. Above Dee's head was a tangle of clothesline with pins attached for hanging black-and-white glossies to dry.

In pitch blackness, Dee took the rolls of film out of their cartridges and wound them around in her stainless steel developing tanks. Then with the light on, she started in on the real work she had ahead of her. If she were going to have the photographs to Sasha by Wednesday, she had a lot to do.

She shook the developing tanks to dislodge bubbles from the film, gave each roll of film a long, drenching bath in developing solution, then looked through the frames to decide which images to print.

Marc in his soccer uniform, his hands on his hips, stared at her right there, the size of an insect in a tiny frame of film. Just looking at him made her shiver slightly. His presence seemed to invade the privacy of her darkroom. Though she hadn't invited him in, he insisted on being there, taking up image after image on her rolls of film.

Against her better judgment, Dee decided to print one of the shots of Marc. She could avoid him altogether, but he was in practically every shot and she had to have something to give Sasha. Dee chose the very last roll, the one of Marc making the winning goal.

After going through all the long, careful steps, she waited expectantly over the tray of liquid solution and watched the image of Marc emerge gradually on the blank piece of photography paper. First he was a hazy shape. Then specific details came into focus. The number on his jersey. The clench of his fist as he made the kick.

Dee watched his face appear. His eyes. His lips. His chin. Slowly they became clearer, more life-like. Soon everything about him was captured right there on the paper, and as Dee studied his face and his body, all she could think about was how much she wanted to have everything between them just as it had been on Saturday night.

She bit her lip. It took all her determination to keep from starting to cry all over again. She stood up straight and took a deep breath. She couldn't cry all over her negatives.

If strength were ever called for, she told herself, it's time to have it now. Looking at Marc's picture was just the beginning. In a few days she'd run into him at school no matter how hard she might try to avoid him, and she'd have to confront him then. If she allowed herself to cry over a photograph now, what would happen when she saw him in person? No, she had to be brave about all of this. She had to be controlled.

She would hang the picture up to dry and make a few more prints of other highlights of the game. And then she would go to bed and push Marc out of her mind forever.

But Dee shook her head. She knew there wasn't much chance of that. Just looking at Marc's photograph made her realize how much she missed him. She'd give anything to be able to talk with him right now. Anything. Why hadn't she answered the phone?

As she looked down at his face again, she decided that even just being friends with him would be better than not knowing him at all. She didn't want any hostility between them. If the phone rang again tonight, she'd answer it.

Then she remembered that Gloria had said he'd be out with Jenny. He wouldn't call tonight, Dee told herself. She shouldn't get her hopes up.

She listened for the phone anyway. She stayed in her bedroom while she ran her bath, just so she'd hear the phone in case it rang. When she thought she heard Billy talking on the phone in the kitchen, she raced downstairs so quickly she almost fell. But she didn't have to beg him to hang up and free the line. She found him sitting quietly in front of the television. The talking she'd heard had all been in her mind.

For the rest of the night, the phone never rang.

Chapter
22

"Try that again," Woody insisted. "You sound like a trumpet player with mud in his horn."

Ten of the twelve people on the stage giggled at Woody's comment. Michael and Phoebe didn't.

They kept as far away from each other as they could manage during the practice session. And neither of them smiled once at Woody's jokes.

Michael and the rest of the musicians sat in a semicircle in the middle of the stage. Phoebe and the three others in her quartet stood at the front, looking out into the darkness of the theater and waiting for Woody's directions.

Often the singers turned to talk and make suggestions to the orchestra. But Phoebe stood rigidly, her back to them. She knew if she moved her body even a quarter of a turn, she'd be able to see Michael out of the corner of her eye. And she didn't want to catch even the briefest glimpse of him.

Woody started directing the group again. After the musicians played their introduction, the singers launched into "Somewhere a Place for Us" from *West Side Story*.

Wouldn't you know Woody would make us sing something from that musical, Phoebe thought, as she braced herself to sing the words. He hadn't consulted her on the program. He'd just made sure she got the music she needed to learn a couple of weeks ago. She hadn't had the heart to tell him she'd hoped never to hear anything from *West Side Story* again as long as she lived.

And of all the choices, "Somewhere a Place for Us," she thought. There's never a place for us. Not with me and Griffin. Or me and Michael. The song was just the kind of romantic dream people found in musicals. Love just wasn't that easy. Not in real life.

Woody waved his arms around as if he were conducting a chorus of thousands instead of this small group on the Little Theater stage. He was so earnest about what he was doing. In spite of her depression, Phoebe almost wanted to smile. But she didn't.

"Better, better," Woody said. "Now go back to the first few phrases again. You're starting out too slowly."

The orchestra tried again, and Woody finally brought them to a halt. "Great. You've got it." He swept his arms around in a grand gesture of appreciation. "Just look at those guys behind you," he said to the singers. "Be grateful you've got such fine musicians to back you up."

The singers all turned around toward the orchestra — except for Phoebe. She stood there, stiff and proud.

"Look, Phoebe," Woody said. "Let's give them a hand."

Since Woody singled her out, Phoebe knew she couldn't just stand there facing north, like someone on a ship lost at sea. She turned toward the musicians and her eyes were drawn to Michael, sitting stiffly, his cello propped between his knees. The minute their eyes met, both of them looked away.

He seems so sad, Phoebe thought. She couldn't stop herself from glancing at him again. Their eyes locked a second time. They looked away again.

Phoebe could tell Michael was upset. His cheeks were set hard. His usual cheerful smile had gotten lost somewhere. She wondered if he were trying to control his feelings as much as she was.

Maybe she should talk to him, Phoebe thought. Maybe they could say enough to each other to clear up their misery and be friends at least. Avoiding each other was not going to be easy for the rest of the year.

But as Phoebe considered the possibility of trying to start up a conversation with him, she realized she didn't really know what she would say. He had been so closed-minded on Saturday.

He hadn't understood the way she cared or the effort she was making. He'd taken her attempt to make things better, and thrown it back into her face.

No, there was no sense trying to talk to him again. It wouldn't do any good. He was impossible, and she may as well face that cold, hard fact and try to accept it. If he'd hurt her so badly once, he'd do it again. And she wasn't about to leave herself open for his anger and rejection again. She preferred ignoring him — even if it meant doing so until graduation.

"That's enough for today," Woody said as he walked around on stage among the orchestra and singers. "You've done a great job learning the music. And I think with a few more rehearsals, we'll have this show ready to knock the socks off of everyone at the Arts Fair."

He was soon drowned out by the sound of everyone packing up to leave. The musicians snapped and zipped their instrument cases shut. The singers gathered up their books, coats, and sheet music.

"See you on Saturday," Woody said, and walked toward the director's cubicle behind the stage.

" 'Bye, Woody." Phoebe called and waved to him.

She put her music into her backpack, swung it over her shoulder, and headed with the rest of the students outside into the cold. As she walked, she looked straight ahead without a glance to either side that might bring Michael into view.

Phoebe was glad to be outside. The cold felt good. She pulled the collar of her coat up closer around her neck, and started walking quickly. Just as she took a step, however, she bumped into someone walking in the same direction.

She looked to her right to see who it was, and her body stiffened.

"Excuse me," Phoebe said, and moved away.

"That's okay," Michael said.

For Phoebe, looking at him across the stage had been bad enough. But actually hearing his voice was even worse. It made her wince with a sadness she never would have thought possible after all her anger last weekend. Why did Michael have to sound so vulnerable? Something about his voice seemed as hurt to Phoebe as her own feelings.

"I didn't mean to ram into you," she said, knowing she was just stalling and trying to think of some way to keep talking to him.

"I wasn't looking where I was going," he said.

"It was my fault."

"No. Mine."

"This is crazy," Phoebe said. She and Michael had never been this polite before.

Michael cleared his throat as if he were about to make a formal announcement. "Do you want to go walk by the river?" he asked.

"Yes," Phoebe answered, her voice quivering slightly.

They walked all the way to the river without saying a word. Each time their arms or shoulders touched accidentally, they both took quick steps to separate. When they reached the bridge, they stood together for several minutes, looking down into the icy darkness of the water.

The coldness of the river wasn't all that different from the chill between her and Michael, Phoebe thought. She leaned her elbows on the brick wall at the bridge's edge and peered down into the depths below. It would be months before summer came and sunshine would sparkle warmly again on the rippling surface of the water. By then her senior year would almost be over, and she and Michael might never even see each other again unless they made the effort. They'd have no more chance meetings like today outside the Little Theater. She wouldn't sit with him and the rest of the crowd at lunch anymore.

Phoebe didn't think she'd ever felt so sad before. Even if she were angry at Michael, even if he had been horrible, even if he were the most stubborn person she'd ever known, she still cared for him. She could hardly stand the thought of graduating and never seeing him again.

"Michael," she said.

"It's okay, Phoebe." He put his arm around her. "I was just thinking the same thing."

"How do you know what I was thinking?"

"I don't know exactly, but I could tell a lot from your face."

"And what could you tell?"

"That you'd be as sorry as I would if we never got back together."

Phoebe smiled at him. "That was sort of what I was thinking."

"I was thinking even more than that," Michael added.

"What?"

"That I'm sorry I blew up at you on Saturday."

"I'm sorry, too." Phoebe leaned closer to him. "I didn't mean to upset you by what I said. I was just trying to make things better. Really."

"You don't have to do that, Phoebe. There couldn't be anything better for me than you."

Phoebe felt tears welling up in her eyes. As they started sneaking down her cheeks, Michael wiped them away with the tips of his fingers.

"I want to say something one last time, and that's got to be the end of it," he said.

"What?"

"That Leah was just someone I knew before you and I were even together. You're the only girl friend I want."

Michael wrapped his arms around Phoebe and kissed her gently on the lips. "I love you," he whispered.

Phoebe buried her face into the warm protection of his chest. "I love you, too," she said.

As they stood there holding each other, a car whizzed past them on the bridge, full of teenage boys honking the horn, and shouting boisterously. Phoebe and Michael looked at them and laughed.

"I guess the people you love aren't interchangeable," she said. "I should have learned that from my experience with Griffin, but I was just so scared it would be different for you."

"It seems to me I said the same thing to you not long ago," Michael said. His mouth turned up into a broad grin. "You may be a little slow, Phoebe, but you do learn eventually."

Chapter
23

"Dee, these photos are fantastic!" Sasha said. She bent over the pictures Dee had spread out on her desk in *The Red and the Gold* office. "You're the best photographer we've ever had!"

"Thanks, Sasha," Dee said. Sasha's enthusiasm pleased her. If Marc were going to go back to Jenny, then at least Dee had her work with the newspaper to keep her busy. It would be a good focus for her life right now.

"You have such an eye for the right shots," Sasha added. "And you've captured the action so well."

"There was lots of action to capture."

"Wasn't there? It was a great game. We've got to be sure to use this picture." Sasha pointed to the one of Marc. "Since his goal won the game, he deserves the credit."

Dee nodded agreement without saying anything. She didn't want to get started talking about Marc, even in a polite conversation over his photograph. The less said about him, the better.

Sasha picked up all the photographs and slid them into a large manilla envelope. "I forgot to tell you, Dee," she said. "Marc came looking for you here at lunch. He's really worried about you."

"Me?" Dee asked, surprised.

"He said he'd been trying to find you everywhere."

"Oh." Dee knew she could talk to Sasha about Marc. But it would be too upsetting. She couldn't do it now.

"Is something wrong between you two?" Sasha asked finally.

"No, everything's fine," Dee lied, holding back her tears, and rushing out of Sasha's office to her locker. She still had the books on cheerleading and soccer to take back to the library. They had been sitting there in the bottom under her paint set for several days. And when she looked at them now, they seemed almost like an affront.

The cheerleading book didn't make her feel too bad. She'd practically forgotten all about her fall. But the soccer book felt heavy and cold in her hands. She opened the cover and glanced at the photographs inside. Just a week ago she'd been poring over every word in the book, trying to learn the rules of soccer, so she could take better photographs and follow the game. She'd also thought it would be nice to be informed about something so important to Marc. What a joke.

She decided to drop the books off this very afternoon, and get them out of her locker once and for all. Maybe being rid of them would purge her of bad memories. But Dee suspected it would take a lot more than just returning a few books before she'd be happy again.

She closed her locker door and walked slowly toward the library. When she got to the librarian's desk, she found Fiona, checking out a book on ballet.

"Hi, Dee. What books did you take out?" Fiona asked, trying to see the covers.

"Just a couple of books I'm finished with."

Suddenly, Dee felt the tears she'd been trying to hold back all day threatening to overflow.

Fiona frowned at her. "Dee," she said as she tucked her ballet book under her arm and took her friend by the elbow. "Let's go outside."

As they walked together out to Dee's bicycle, they ran into Laurie, who was on her way to the parking lot.

"What's wrong, Dee?" Laurie asked immediately when she saw how upset Dee looked.

Dee sniffled and Fiona didn't know what to say.

"Can I help?" Laurie asked, walking beside them.

Only a few cars and bicycles were left so late in the day. The air smelled of tires and car oil. In the distance Dee heard the shouts of the soccer team. Marc was probably out there on the field. The very thought was painful.

"What's going on, Dee?" Fiona asked again.

"You've got to tell us. We want to help."

"I'm okay," Dee answered.

The shakiness of Dee's voice told Laurie and Fiona otherwise. "We're not going to just stand here and watch you fall apart. Come on. You'll feel better if you talk about it," Fiona said. "Does it have to do with Marc?"

"I don't know," Dee answered. "I mean, I guess so." She shook her head. "I don't know."

"You're not making a whole lot of sense, Dee," Laurie said.

"I can't make sense if I don't understand what's going on."

"What's happened?" Fiona asked. She put her arm around Dee protectively. "He's obviously hurt you."

"He hasn't, exactly."

Laura and Fiona waited silently for Dee to explain.

Everyone would find out about Marc and Jenny soon enough, Dee thought. She may as well tell them. What good did it do to hold everything in anyway?

"On Monday . . . I ran . . . into Gloria Macmillan," Dee explained halting between sobs. "Just before school started." Gradually, with words of encouragement from Fiona and Laurie, Dee got out the whole story.

"But don't you see what's going on?" Laurie asked.

"Just that Marc's going back to Jenny."

"No, that's not it at all," Laurie said. "Gloria's making everything up. Remember what we were saying at the sub shop? You know how she ruined my campaign. And Jeremy was mad at her for weeks after she tried to wreck his video tape. I know just what she's doing. She's trying to hurt you."

"Why me? I hardly even know her."

"She wants to get back at all of us because we aren't friends with her," Laurie insisted. She had once been in that same position herself, and she hadn't acted any better than Gloria. "She probably figures if she can hurt one of us, she can get us all somehow."

Dee wished she could believe her. She pressed her hand against her forehead to think more clearly.

"Marc really cares about you, Dee," Fiona put in. "I'm sure of that. I can tell by how he acts. He's been crazy about you since that first day in the sub shop."

"But he told me himself that Jenny wanted to get back together with him," Dee argued. "He must be having a hard time forgetting her. They were together for a whole year."

"But Marc broke up with Jenny. They weren't right for each other. Anybody can see it's over," Fiona said. "You're just refusing to listen to the truth because you're scared."

"Scared?"

"Well, wary. You're afraid to really care about him, or fight for him because you think he'll hurt you."

"He already has," Dee said, frowning.

"No, he hasn't. Gloria Macmillan has. And we

all know how mixed-up she is," Laurie said.

Dee sighed. "I'd give anything if you were right."

Laurie put her hands on her hips. "I *am* right."

"I don't know." Dee shook her head.

"You need to talk with Marc and find out for yourself," Fiona encouraged.

"I'm afraid to see him. I don't want him to tell me he's going back to Jenny."

"But he won't tell you that," Laurie said.

Dee still wasn't sure. No matter what Laurie and Fiona said, how could she believe them? Dee remembered the look on Jenny's face after the soccer game. Jenny, Dee could tell, would do anything to get Marc back. And how could Dee stop her after all the time she and Marc had known each other — even before Dee ever got to Kennedy High?

She grabbed the handlebars of her bicycle and steered it out of the rack.

"Thanks," Dee said. "You've been good friends to listen to all this."

"Just talk to him," Laurie called after her. "I'm sure you'll get this straightened out."

Dee smiled halfheartedly at her friends and started pedaling home. Her ankle didn't really hurt anymore. It was completely healed. Dee wondered how long it would take her feelings to heal if Gloria was telling the truth. And in her heart, she had to believe Gloria was right about Marc.

When she had barely left the school parking lot, she had a sudden impulse to ride by the soccer field. Maybe Marc would be out there kicking the ball along the grass. She could start getting used to seeing him, she thought, and practice looking right at him without getting upset. But she knew she really wanted to go by the soccer field simply to get a glimpse of him.

Knowing she was hidden from the soccer team by the bleachers at the edge of the field, Dee leaned her bicycle against them and walked cautiously over to get a closer look at the players. They were running up and down the field, stealing the ball back and forth, shouting to each other.

She searched everywhere for Marc, but didn't see him. Standing on her tiptoes, she peered over the top of a row of seats and scanned the entire field. No one was sitting on the sidelines anywhere. Marc was gone.

"Dee," a voice shouted behind her.

Without even turning around, she knew it was Marc.

She turned to face him. "Hi," she said, trying to steady her voice.

Marc stopped in front of her.

"I've been looking for you for two whole days. Where have you been?"

"Where I always am," Dee answered steadily. "At home. At school."

She didn't want to hear about Jenny Woods. Not here. She started toward her bicycle. "I've got to get home. I'm late."

"Wait a minute." Marc blocked her way and put his arms on her shoulders. "You can't just leave now after I've finally found you."

So this was it. Dee braced herself.

"I called you three times yesterday. Twice in the afternoon. And once right after dinner before my mom and I went to the mall." Marc dropped his hands from her shoulders. "I looked all over for you at school yesterday and today." Marc paused for a moment and frowned. "If you're avoiding me, Dee, I'd rather you just came out and told me."

"Of course I'm avoiding you," Dee said in a flash of emotion. "What else am I supposed to do?"

She was glad to be confronting him now. They'd have to have it out.

"What do you mean?"

"If you're going back to Jenny, then say so. It doesn't matter to me."

"Jenny? Are you kidding? What ever gave you that idea?"

Dee clenched her fists at her sides.

"I told you last Saturday that it was over between me and Jenny. I have no intention of getting together with her again."

"I heard you did."

"From whom?"

"Gloria Macmillan. Jenny told her. She said you'd told her, too."

Marc's eyes narrowed angrily. "Listen, Dee, if there's going to be anything between us, we've got to trust each other. Surely you couldn't listen to Gloria Macmillan instead of me."

"How can we trust each other if you're back together with Jenny?"

"I told you." Marc spoke slowly and deliberately. "I'm not getting back with her. Can't you get that through your head? It's you I want. I told you that on Saturday. I meant it, Dee. You've got to believe me."

Marc stared down at her face for a moment silently. Then his eyes softened. "A guy would have to be crazy not to fall in love with you, Dee. And I'm not crazy." He paused. "Except maybe about you."

The smile on his face looked so sincere. Dee couldn't fight what he told her anymore. It had to be the truth.

When he bent down to kiss her, she responded, all her hurt and anger melting away in that one kiss.

"I love you, Dee," he whispered against her cheek. "And if you don't believe me, then there's nothing I can do about it."

"I believe you." Dee said in a low voice as she held him tightly. He kissed her softly again.

Finally, he pulled back from her and grinned. "Now that we've got that settled, I have to get back to practice. I was talking to the coach about recruiting new players. He wouldn't take to my disappearing for very long."

"You'd better get going, then. . . ." Dee said.

Marc bent down and kissed her again.

"I'll call you tonight," he said as he took off toward the field. He waved to her as she got on her bicycle.

Dee got a last good look at the team as she pedaled along the street, then turned toward home. Even in the cold November air, her lips felt warm from Marc's kiss. She could still feel just where his hands had rested on her shoulders. Everything was fine again. And she felt so happy she wanted to shout her joy to the clear blue sky.

Coming Soon . . .
Couples #17
DANCE WITH ME

All morning long, Fiona continued to hope that Jonathan wouldn't show up. But at the stroke of noon, the doorbell rang twice. Fiona grimaced at her reflection in the hall mirror, brushed a fleck of mascara off her cheek, and hurried down the hall. She paused with one hand on the door-knob and took a deep breath. She didn't want Jonathan to get the idea that she was the least bit nervous about this idiotic blind date. She promised herself, one last time, to be nice to Jeremy's friend — no matter how boring and difficult the afternoon turned out to be.

She flung open the door and suddenly she forgot her carefully prepared introduction. Fiona found herself looking up into a pair of startlingly penetrating gray eyes. He didn't look the least bit like the Hollywood hero Jeremy had described. He looked more like the David Bowie poster

Fiona had over her bed, even though he *was* wearing a soft Indiana Jones-style hat. The gray felt made his eyes seem even grayer.

As she watched him watch her, the expression in his eyes changed from friendly to surprised to something that made her spine tingle. She shivered and forced herself to look away.

"Uh, I'll get my jacket," she mumbled, and stepped back into the hall. Fiona grabbed her short denim jacket off the coatrack, and tugged it over her long sweater. Suddenly, she remembered she hadn't introduced herself. She didn't even know if this was Jonathan.

"I'm Fiona," she said, noticing for the first time his awful, moth-eaten raccoon coat. It looked like something her grandfather might have worn to a 1930's rugby game. It was disgusting.

He shifted his gaze away from her face and intently studied the porch railing, then his loafers. Finally he focused on a point over Fiona's right shoulder. She turned around nervously, wondering what he was looking at. He seemed to be studying the brass numbers tacked to the shingles.

"I'm Jonathan Preston," he said sticking out his hand. His voice *was* the same warm friendly voice she remembered from the phone. Fiona shook his hand. It was firm and dry and very pleasant to touch, but when the deep fur cuff on his sleeve brushed her wrist, she cringed. She suddenly didn't know if she was relieved or disappointed that this really was her blind date.